A Festive Verisimilitude

Paul R Stanton

Ukiyoto Publishing

All global publishing rights are held by

Ukiyoto Publishing

Published in 2023

Content Copyright © Paul R Stanton

ISBN 9789360162344

www.ukiyoto.com

This book is dedicated to Chapter 8.

Contents

Jonathan Peaty

Being the 18th December

The old man sat just to the left of the entrance to Charing Cross train station. It was a spot he felt comfortable with. It was a spot where he knew he wouldn't be under the feet of the general public and commuters. It was a spot where he was just apparent enough to everyone passing, that is either going in or out of the station. It was a good spot and it was his spot, and he treasured it. It was hard to imagine, given the present circumstances, that by the end of the day he would never ever be begging here again. In fact, he would never be begging anywhere.

He got to his feet and then rearranged the piece of cardboard upon which he had been sitting, once again. This was something he did every twenty minutes, or so; he did this not because he found his position uncomfortable, no, not at all, but more because it gave him something to do, it gave him an excuse to stretch his ageing limbs a little.

Having repositioned himself, he leant forward slightly and looked dolefully into the chipped, white enamel mug he had placed before him on the ground. This was what he used to collect any donations that were likely to come his way throughout the day. Some days were better than others. Looking at the meagre amount he had so far collected that morning, he felt that perhaps today was not going to be a good day. Though you could never tell. People sometimes surprised you, and things may pick up a little later; sometimes they did, sometimes they didn't. It was all pot-luck at the end of the day. With his old gnarled hands, he lifted the mug and tipped the contents out onto the ground before him. There was a total of one pound and thirty-six pence, exactly. Better than nothing, he thought, though it was hardly likely to provide him with a hearty breakfast at Bertram's Hotel. Slowly picking up the coins, he replaced them into the mug and then gave it a shake just for good measure. It did no harm to remind people that he was still there (though in this instance it elicited no more than one or two hostile stares). Oh well, as he said, it was still early days. Hopefully things would pick up later.

Looking up at the sky caused him to frown a little. There were dark clouds on the horizon. That meant either rain, hail or even worse – snow. It was certainly getting cold enough for the latter. Well, he would have to wait and see. At a pinch, he could always go inside. The railway staff generally didn't like that and often moved him on when he did, but he found that if he continued to move around then he had more of a chance of staying in the relative warmth of the station for a little while longer. And at his time of life, it was greatly appreciated.

Sighing, he watched as the people came and went throughout the day. All of them moving at such a frenetic pace, all seemingly trying to overtake their own lives. Not an enviable position to be in – though it had to be said, the greater proportion of them were in a far better position than he was because of it. Sleeping rough had altogether debilitating effects upon his well-being, and not to mention his state of mental health. At night the cold and the damp got so bad at times, that it felt as if it were creeping into the very marrow of his bones. In the mornings, it often proved to be very difficult to move at all. This meant he was obliged to massage his arms and legs thoroughly, just to get some life back into them. To be honest, he wasn't at all sure just how much longer he could put up with this sort of existence. It would undoubtedly be the death of him. But then that was life, wasn't it, or so they said? He thought that there had to be something better than all this. Though, saying that he had thought this many times, and heaven knows, it wouldn't have to be a marked improvement to make his life a little more tolerable. But what was he thinking? How silly. Life couldn't ever get any better for him, and to think otherwise was nothing more than a pipe-dream. He smiled to himself and then chuckled, he must be getting senile and becoming a fantasist in his old age. It never paid to have ideas above your station in life, especially if you were living on the streets, as he was. Everyone knew who you were, they knew your place in society, and so did you and it was generally accepted by all parties. You were scum, human flotsam, detritus, that part of the underbelly of humanity that people usually acknowledged and then moved on. It was easier that way. As long as they weren't in your shoes, then life was generally good. A few coins here occasionally did wonders to appease the old conscience. Anyhow, most of the homeless probably deserved it, didn't they? They were either druggies, alcoholics, lunatics, or even an admixture of all three. And what of those with mental issues, or those who were not able to lead a normal existence within the mainstream of society? Well, surely that's up to the government to do something about it, or at the very least the local authority? In fact, the government probably already did, only those who were homeless didn't want the help and actually resented it. Either way, most people went about their business knowing that there was very little they personally could do about things. That would be the responsibility of someone else. It had become an on-going cliché; someone else would be dealing with it. And so, nothing ever changed and nothing ever would. It was the same, year in and year out, and it had been the same since time immemorial.

The old man sighed with the knowledge, his thoughts weighing heavily upon his mind, then they were suddenly interrupted by a young woman who was standing there before him. She had a kindly face and was clutching a hot drink in a polystyrene cup.

"Hello," she said, smiling a little nervously. "I took the liberty of getting you a cup of hot chocolate. I thought as the weather was cold it might warm you up a bit. There are two sugars. I hope that's all right?"

She looked at him expectantly. People rarely stopped to speak nowadays, not even those who were kind enough to donate to his cause. They probably didn't want to run the risk of catching penury, or an impoverished disease.

The old man smiled in return. He was genuinely grateful and appreciated the kindness she had shown him.

"That's most kind of you, my dear," he said, taking the polystyrene cup from her and immediately appreciating the warmth it gave.

"Are you going to be all right?" she asked. There was a genuine concern in her voice. It touched him deeply.

"Oh yes," he replied. "I'm fine. Absolutely fine. Don't fret yourself. I've survived this long against all the odds. And there's still a bit of life left in the old dog yet. Not a great deal, admittedly, but a smidgeon. And anyway, it will soon be Christmas, won't it? That's always something to look forward to. I'm told it might snow soon. Who knows?"

"But don't you have anywhere to go?" she asked, which caused him to nod in agreement.

"Somewhere to go? Why, indeed, I do," he replied, smiling broadly. "It's a large accommodation, curiously enough and it's open twenty-four seven, three hundred and sixty-five days of the year, and it's called 'La Streets'."

The young woman looked puzzled by this. She was unsure as to precisely what he meant by it.

"La Streets? I don't think I know it," she said. "Where exactly is it?"

The old man sipped on the hot chocolate she had given him before replying.

"Why? It's everywhere I choose to rest my head, my dear," he replied, and gestured to the pavement before him and then laughed loudly at the irony of it all.

It took a brief moment for the young woman to fully comprehend the old man's sense of humour. When she did, she didn't find it funny, but looked totally horrified at the thought of it.

"At Christmas time?" she asked. "Surely, there must be other places you can go to at this time of year, I mean other than sleeping on the streets?"

"Yes, there are," he admitted. "Though to be honest, most people usually tell me to go to hell. It's not overly comfortable, or so I'm led to believe, but warm nevertheless. It would certainly keep the chill out, wouldn't it?"

Again, he laughed loudly.

The young woman really had no idea what to say to him. Her compassion shone through, but then so did her impotence at being able to do anything about it. At last, she took out her purse and quickly went through it. Pulling from it a single note, she placed it carefully in his cup.

"Look, I don't have much – but you are welcome to what I have. I think your need is far greater than mine. I'm sorry, but I have to get back to work now. If I don't, I'll be in for it with my boss. I do hope that you find somewhere to go." She smiled warmly, turned and then left, leaving the old man to watch her studiously as she walked away.

"A genuinely compassionate soul," he mumbled to himself. "One to watch out for there, I think." And then went back to sipping his hot chocolate.

Later that same day, once the young woman had arrived home, she went through her purse in order to locate her front door key. She was altogether perplexed to see that it now contained - four freshly minted fifty-pound notes, which certainly hadn't been there when she left out that morning. No-one had had access to her purse during the day, so where had it come from? It was a mystery, and one that she would never get to the bottom of.

The day moved slowly on, people in their hundreds came and went, and the old man continued to wait patiently. As forecast earlier in the day, his cup had slowly begun to fill up. At the last count there was now in excess of thirty pounds in there. At Christmas time people were usually a little more charitable, even if they chose not to speak. He had no complaints. Such was life.

For the past hour or so, he had noticed a young man standing just across the way from where he sat. He appeared to be taking an unhealthy interest in him, or more to the point, an unhealthy interest in his white enamel mug. Every now and then he would catch the young man out of the corner of his eye staring at it in an unhealthy way. Thinking it prudent to move it a little closer, the old man did so. You couldn't be too careful nowadays. He looked up, just in time to see the young man avert his gaze. It could be just a coincidence, though it might be wise to keep an eye on him, he thought. There may be nothing in it, but then you would never quite knew.

The day progressively moved into late afternoon and the greater majority of the working population had now passed through the station and had returned home. The old man thought it best to finish for the day and make his way back to where he had secreted what few belongings he possessed. And they were precious few. Collecting the contents of the enamel mug, he pushed them down firmly into his coat pocket, where he knew they would be safe. It hadn't been such a bad day after all, he thought. Slowly he got to his feet. That wasn't easy, as his legs had become slightly numb through all the sitting. Once he was steady again, he gradually began to make his way down Villiers Street. Not far down there was a turning just to the right. It was more of a rear entry point to the back of Charing Cross Station, where deliveries were made. Very few people used it, but he found it useful to store his few odds and ends there. At the end of the day, it was all locked up, so sleeping there wasn't really an option; which was a pity as it was quite dry and enclosed and would have remained fairly warm.

He soon found his sleeping bag and other items he had left there earlier in the day, and was in the process of collecting his things together, when a noise from behind caused him to turn. Standing before him was the young man he had spotted earlier, the same one who had been watching him intently for most of the afternoon.

"What do you want?" asked the old man, tremulously, knowing exactly where this was likely to lead.

As there was no-one else about, the young man came straight to the point, feeling completely confident in his purpose.

"I want whatever was in that mug of yours, gramps. So, hand it over and be quick about it and there won't be any trouble."

In a panic the old man's hand automatically went to his coat pocket, where he had collected all the money that day. He gripped it tightly and hung on with all his strength and had no intention of giving it up without putting up some stiff resistance.

"No, you can't have it! It's mine!" he cried in alarm. "I need it. I'm old! Leave me alone! Please leave me alone!"

Moving forward, the young man grabbed the front of his coat and began shaking him fiercely, which caused the old man to drop the objects he had been holding.

"I'm not in the mood for games, grandpa!" he shouted, menacingly. "I don't want to hurt you, but I will, unless you hand it over and quick!" The old man was slight, and weighing little quickly fell to his knees, but even so he still resolutely hung onto his coat pocket. He was determined not to give up his hard-earned money, without at least putting up a fight of sorts.

"Don't take my money! Please don't take my money!" he begged. "I need it!"

The young man made a grab at the pocket that he knew contained the money he was after. The other tried to grab his hand and prevent him from doing so. This only angered the younger man even more. Raising his fist, he quickly let fly, catching the old man a terrific blow to the side of the head. He fell, blood instantly trickling from a severe cut that had now opened up upon his cheek. Leaving the old man helpless, the young man then quickly went through his pocket, emptying the contents and filling his own, all the while ignoring the pleading and protestations of the older man. Once he had taken every penny the old man had, he quickly turned to leave. It crossed his mind that it had been a good few minutes' work. He grinned, feeling more than satisfied with himself. If only it was always this easy.

The young man hadn't gone more than a few yards, when he unexpectedly heard a voice calling after him. The voice was deep, commanding and strangely other-worldly. It sent a shiver down his spine that he couldn't account for.

"Jonathan Peaty," it boomed. "I would have words with you."

The voice knew his name. But how was that possible? Turning, he saw that the old man had now totally disappeared, and standing in his place was a much younger man, tall, black beard and very well dressed. The man stared at him; his gaze seemed all consuming. It terrified him, though he didn't know why. There was something supernatural about those eyes, their intensity, that gaze, which caused his blood to freeze in his veins.

The man took a series of quick strides towards him that were unnaturally quick. Jonathan, having seen enough, immediately turned and fled. At least that was his intention. But for some odd reason he was now confronted by a barrier and despite his being able to see through it, as well as being able to view all the people in the street beyond, it allowed him no ingress whatsoever.

It was immovable and wholly impenetrable. He was utterly trapped. Banging frantically on it with his fists, flailing away in rising terror – he then began screaming loudly for all he was worth. Those people beyond paid him no heed, almost as if he were not there at all. Why couldn't they see him?

He then felt a hand descend upon his shoulder, and all at once he fell to his knees. Totally immured, it felt as if the very life had been drawn from him. Looking up he saw the man peering down at him – those terrible eyes, blazing and insightful, penetrating down to his very soul. He wanted to run, but had his life depended on it, he could not have done so.

The man smiled and then lifted him up by his arm. Jonathan Peaty was utterly helpless to resist. And then the man spoke again.

"Well, Jonathan, lets tarry awhile, shall we? I really think it's time we had a little chat," he said, leading him gently away. Having located some large industrial containers, that were ideal for sitting on, the man placed Jonathan upon one and then took up a position next to him. "Before we begin, Jonathan, I think I ought to introduce myself," he said. "Now, I have to say, if I was totally honest with you, I rarely get to this stage with people. Although, I usually endeavour to give folk the benefit of the doubt, that is when I am able to do so, I only ever do that on the basis that I remain anonymous; that is, I am completely under wraps, as it were. However, in your case I seriously think that you knowing who I am will do your cause a whole lot of good; ultimately, that is. Do you understand what I am telling you?" Jonathan, without voice, nodded. "That's excellent my boy. I feel we are getting to understand one another right from the off. And there's no better way to start an in-depth conversation in my opinion. Very well, I am commonly known as the Devil; though I do have various other titles, but ultimately, they are only labels and serve little purpose here, so the Devil it will remain."

By now Jonathan was sitting with his mouth agape, in near catatonia, not being able to utter so much as a sound, for he knew that the man's words were true. He was in fact the Devil, the actual Devil. This suited the Devil admirably. There were few things he loathed more than being interrupted when he was in full flow.

"I have to say, Jonathan, that since I first spotted you earlier in the day, and being aware of your intentions, it was my sole intention to consign you to hell for what you meant to do. And I seriously believe you deserved it, too: you have shown callous, wanton greed, and little or no compassion for your fellow man. This, along with a stark unwillingness to even try and oppose the downside to your nature, left me in two minds about you, my boy. Anything and everything that would usually consign anyone to the fiery pit, and good old eternal torment and damnation, then you were the perfect candidate. Then, I thought to myself, well he isn't all bad, is he? Ninety-nine point nine-nine-nine per cent recurring, yes, but not totally rotten to the core. And had I not seen that small spark, that slight vestige in you that said "Give this kid a break" you would be roasting merrily right now, even as we speak. Are you with me on that one?"

Again, Jonathan nodded mutely.

"Tres bien, mon ami, tres bien. Now, I have to admit that we do have a slight problem here, not unsolvable I have to say, but a problem none-the-less; and that problem is – should I endeavour to extract a promise from you that you will, in the future, turn over a new leaf and never in the whole of your life do anything like this again, then you will probably go back on your word and do something equally as bad. Would you agree with me and say that just about sums it all up?"

There was more nodding.

"That's what I thought. So, as I can't abide backsliders, I have chosen a fate for you that will, should you go the distance, and you'll not find it easy, believe me, but should you do so then it will elicit a second chance for you. Are you keeping up with me here, Jonathan?"

Again, more profuse nodding.

"That's what I like to hear. I'm beginning to think that you may be my kind of a guy. Well, no doubt you have often heard the expression 'To be in another man's shoes,' yes? (More nodding). Admirable, truly admirable. You see, I knew you had it in you. So, that being agreed upon, it just behooves me to do the deed. Don't worry, it won't hurt. Though thinking about it, yes it will, it will hurt quite a lot actually – but heck, what's a little pain amongst friends, eh? No more than few kazillion nerve endings going ape-shit, ha ha? Okay, here is my proposition. Are you ready?"

Jonathan nodded, yet again, without knowing what he was letting himself in for.

"Right, hang on to your hat my friend, for what I propose entails you taking my place. Not as the Devil, of course. Trust me you couldn't hack it not for a minute. You will take my place as the old beggar. You may see it as a way of serving your sentence, your penance, giving you the opportunity to do something right for once, instead of constantly being on the take. In this undertaking I will bequeath to you everything that I had – and that includes the money you extracted from me earlier. You may keep it with my blessing. Use it wisely. It isn't easy to come by, believe me."

Jonathan at once began to shake, quite violently and involuntarily; though despite being terrified, it was not fear that brought it about. He felt as though his whole being was suddenly altering, his bodily atoms taking on a whole new different form. He began to shrink down, and at once became aware of intense bodily pain, a pain that wracked him all over. Then his eyesight quickly began to deteriorate, causing him to squint in order to focus properly. Holding up his hands in front of his face, he was horrified to see knobbly calluses that now beset them, and what's more – they hurt, they really hurt bad! Dear God, this couldn't be happening to him? But it was. In less time than it takes to tell, Jonathan Peaty had been transformed into the old beggar he had only just recently robbed. This was something out of his worst nightmares. As he looked up, he could just make out the Devil standing before him. He looked altogether very pleased with himself. Jonathan opened his mouth to plead for forgiveness, but the hoarseness that issued forth caused him to hesitate. He didn't recognise his own voice. It wasn't his own voice.

"Please – you can't leave me like this!" he cried. "I didn't mean it – I'll put things right, I promise! I will!"

"Ah, if I told you Jonathan, the times I have heard that particular supplication down the years. It's always so easy after the event now, isn't it? But I want you to see your current predicament as the soil in which you will spiritually grow and bloom. Anyway, I really must be going – people to see, places to go etc. etc. And not forgetting the most important thing here, it's nearly Christmas. I absolutely adore Christmas, don't you? Though perhaps less so in your current guise, I'd imagine."

The Devil turned to go. Jonathan, lurched forward in his panic and made to grab the Devil's coat. His hands met nothing and he fell to his knees, causing the Devil to turn.

"Don't get up," he said. "And you really need to get that gash on your cheek seen to. It's a nasty contusion you have there. Looks like someone has given you a thorough beating. A simply deplorable act, especially towards the elderly, don't you know? What's the world coming to, eh? Absolutely deplorable."

Jonathan watched in horror as his persecutor disappeared from view. Getting to his feet as fast as his body would allow, he hurriedly followed after him. Once in the street he looked about, expecting to see the Devil just ahead of him. It came as a soul numbing shock to see that in fact he was nowhere to be seen. He had thoroughly disappeared.

After word

On the run up to Christmas, Jonathan could be seen hanging around the station, especially during the day light hours. He spent most of his time either begging, asking for hand-outs, or engaging those in conversation, at least those people who would take the time to listen to his near hysterical rants. "The Devil did this to me!" he would tell them, time and time again. And strangely enough no-one believed him.

The Nameless Horror of Berkeley Square

Being the 19th December – a.m.

The weather was decidedly chilly that morning and there was talk of possible snow later. The prospect pleased the Devil immeasurably; and what with Christmas, itself, being on the horizon, it would be true to say that Old Nick was in his element.

That particular morning, he had a singular purpose in mind. It had to be said, the purpose in question was something he had had a mind to do for quite some time – for well over sixty years, to be more exact. It could have been pointed out by those who, 'weren't in the know' to have been somewhat egregious of him, but he knew better, and was altogether aware of the more archaic interpretation of the word. And naturally, it went without saying, that no-one had any idea as to either his schedule, or personal intent. Either way, it was his call, and it was something that he intended to lay to rest that particular morning, come what may. And in a way he was quite looking forward to it. A minor imbroglio, admittedly, but one that would soon be laid to rest.

Taking out the small note book that he always carried with him, he opened it and began flicking through its pages.

"Oh, I missed that," he muttered absently, and taking out a stubby pencil, placed a small tick by the name of Jonathan Peaty. A good result there, he thought, and snapping the notebook shut again, dismissed the episode from his mind altogether. He then consulted his pocket watch, realised that he was now running a little late, and quickly increased his pace. It would be true to say that it wasn't quite a run, as that was altogether an anathema to him, but it definitely fell into the category of a slow sprint. Crossing the street, he began meandering his way through a number of side streets, until he at last arrived at his port of call. Straight away he espied the group of people he was due to meet that morning: They were Walkers - that is, folk that go on privately conducted walks, such as 'The Jack the Ripper Walk', or 'The Charles Dickens Walk.' All very popular, according to the vox populi, or so he had been led to believe. This particular walk was called 'Ghosts of Old London,' and the Devil was quite looking forward to it, that was in his own idiosyncratic way.

There was a total of eighteen people all told, in the group, including himself when he arrived. These were, in the main, elderly and middle-aged folk. It had to be said, he felt quite at home with them given his longevity.

"He's running a little late, himself," said an elderly woman, who had watched him arrive. "Which was good for you, or you might have missed us, mightn't you? Apparently, he's getting changed into his costume, in that small café over there. He apologised to everyone and said that they had mislaid it, and it has taken a bit of time to locate it. No doubt someone had been tidying up and they've gone and put it somewhere. He's not happy about it, I know that much. Kicked up an almighty fuss when he found out what they had done. Mind you, they don't charge him for looking after it, so he can't say too much, can he? Still, he was rather put out by it."

"No, I don't imagine he can," returned the Devil, with a smile. "Still, it heightens the tension a tad, don't you think? All standing around here, I mean, with baited breath, wondering what ghostly marvels he intends to regale us with throughout the day. I can hardly contain myself at the thought of it."

The woman laughed. It was a spirited laugh that seemed to reflect her personality well.

"I'm Edie, by the way," said the woman. "And this is my husband, Clive." Clive looked rather taciturn, and glum, and merely nodded by way of introduction. He was obviously a man of few words and preferred to leave the small talk to his wife, and she was seemingly more than happy to oblige.

"I'm Nick," said the Devil. "Very pleased to make your acquaintance, I'm sure."

"Have you paid, yet?" she asked. "Only we always pay in advance, as it's slightly cheaper that way?"

The Devil held up a newly printed five-pound note.

"All ready and willing," he said. "Galvanized, and ready for the off, as it were. Exactly where might we be going first; do you happen to know?"

A large portly gentleman, standing next to him and over hearing his question, piped up.

"It's always the same. He never changes his routine, not ever. And I've been on a few."

"That's true," confirmed Edie. "But we don't mind. This is our seventh time on this walk."

"Eighth!" corrected Clive.

"Is it? Are you sure? I could have sworn it was only seven."

"It's eight!" barked Clive, and having made his point returned to a moody and sulky silence.

"Well – seven or eight. It doesn't really matter, does it? You see that wooden contraption over there? That wooden stand thing, that's all painted in black? Can you see it?"

The Devil said that he could.

"Well, there's leaflets in there. If you look closely, you can see them sticking out of the top. They're free, and they give you all the information you need to know about the walk; the time it starts, each place we're going to, how long it takes to walk there. It's all very well organised, and it also mentions his other walks as well. But we think that this one is the best, "Ghosts of Old London," isn't that right, Clive?"

Clive muttered something unintelligible, leaving the Devil to go and help himself to a leaflet. As he examined it, he saw that the style was set out in a rather garish fashion, which he found altogether too macabre for his personal tastes. No doubt it would appeal to the more sanguine members of the group. The leaflet gave a list of all the places they would visit, at least, that is, would be visiting once Mr Ghoulish had located his costume. That was the name the tour guide had adopted for himself, Mr Ghoulish. The Devil thought it rather tacky. The leaflet read: 'Places of Ghastly Interest' 1. The Grey Lady of Grosvenor Place, 2. The Headless Horror of Torbary Square. This then continued in much the same vein; every now and then the entries being interposed with either a red ink mark (supposedly spilled blood) or an image of a ghost shrieking madly. Vulgar, thought the Devil, decidedly vulgar. Running his finger down the list he at last came to the entry he was looking for: The Nameless Horror of Berkeley Square. Bingo! He tapped the leaflet with a finger, causing the portly gentleman to peer across to see what he was pointing at.

"Is that your favourite then?" he asked. "The Berkeley Square Horror? That's a real spooky one I have to admit? Not a place I would like to spend the night, or anyone here if they were honest. Gives me the creeps just thinking about it. You looking forward to that one?"

The Devil nodded in agreement.

"Yes, I think we can safely say, that I do have a somewhat morbid interest in the place," he admitted. "Ah, and if I am not mistaken, it would seem our Mr Ghoulish has at last finally managed to procure his required attire - be that for good or ill, looking at him, that is."

And, indeed he had. Though it had to be said his overall appearance was altogether bizarre in the extreme, and was purely meant to instil a certain avoir peur into his audience. If nothing else, it caused the Devil to raise an eyebrow or two, and a certain morbid dread overcame him.

Mr Ghoulish was dressed in a black tail coat, that looked way too big for him, along with a top hat. Both his hands and face were daubed in a layer of white pancake, that gave his complexion a bleached look, no doubt to emphasise a deathly corpse-like appearance. To top it all, he wore a long black wig that hung down from under his hat. This was also meant to add to his saturnine façade, but in fact did little other than to make him appear as though he was suffering from some severe psychosis of one sort or another and should be incarcerated for the good of everyone.

"Ooo, isn't he good?" exclaimed Edie, clapping her hands together, almost reverentially, causing the Devil to wonder if perhaps Mr Ghoulish may have a been a favourite nephew of hers.

"He's definitely furtive," he finally muttered beneath his breath. "You're sure he hasn't possibly escaped from some detention centre? And why, I ask, is he carrying that plastic step-up contraption, and why on earth is he walking in that curiously twisted angular gait, rather in the style of Quasimodo from the Hunchback of Notre Dame?"

"Ooh, you'll see," said Edie, pointing. "Just watch him. He's a real pro, isn't he, Clive?"

Clive, not giving a hoot as to whether the man was a pro or not, merely grumped a response, that neither the Devil, nor Edie, could understand. As they continued to watch, it became all too apparent why Mr Ghoulish needed the plastic step-up. He was a rather short individual, so therefore, required it in order to rise above his audience and make himself heard. The Devil couldn't help but think that it detracted from the whole ensemble, and most certainly undermined any chilling aspect that he was meant to portray. But who was he to criticise?

When Mr Ghoulish finally spoke, his voice carried an unusually forced sepulchral timbre. This caused the Devil to wince noticeably with embarrassment, as speaking in a sepulchral timbre was something he knew quite a lot about.

"Please place your money in Mr Ghoulish's box!" he called to the crowd. Those that hadn't paid beforehand moved forward to do just that, the Devil included. As he did so he could see that the small wooden money box was shaped like a tiny coffin, with a slot cut in the lid. Most bizarre, he noted.

When all the payments had been made, Mr Ghoulish addressed the crowd once again, which had now grown to about twenty-five people, all told. He announced loudly that the tour was about to commence, and that those of a delicate disposition had been warned in advance of what might materialise throughout the course of their excursion, and that being the case they may not wish to continue further (no refunds given, of course). Everyone was told to keep together, and if anyone noticed any interlopers who were trying to join them without paying, they were to inform him at once and he would deal with it.

"A question," said the Devil to Edie. Edie was all ears. "In all the times that you and Clive have been on this tour, have either of you ever seen any ghosts, or anything at all that might even be attributed to the supernatural for that matter?"

Edie thought about it at length, then shook her head most emphatically.

"No," she replied. "Well, I mean you wouldn't, would you? Not if you think about it."

"Why, wouldn't you?" he wanted to know.

"It stands to reason, doesn't it? Ghosts don't usually come out during the daytime, do they? I mean, it's just common sense."

And the portly gentleman added.

"That's right. They're more your night time sort, aren't they? It's more natural for them. You see, they like the dark best, so they can frighten people. That's general knowledge."

The Devil nodded in agreement.

"Yes, silly me. I feel that I should have known that," he said. "Well, I feel as though I have learnt something today if nothing else. I shall endeavour to bear it in mind."

And so, the tour began, with Mr Ghoulish enthusiastically leading the way. Every so often he would come to a halt at a prearranged stopping point, clamber up onto the step-up, and entertain the crowd with ghostly stories that were obviously embroidered, or even in some cases, totally made up. The crowd seemed to lap it up, as Mr Ghoulish heightened the atmosphere by gesticulating with his arms, wildly waving them about for dramatic emphasis. The Devil felt a definite yawn coming on. After roughly forty-five minutes of traversing the London streets, he was decidedly losing the will to live and wondered if may be a more direct approach to his current problem might not be a better solution. Eventually, after what seemed an eternity, something the Devil knew quite a lot about, they finally arrived at his reason for being there in the first place: number 50 Berkeley Square – dubbed the most haunted house in London. The building stood before him and beckoned him in. It had been occupied by an antiquarian bookseller for more than seventy years, but in all outward appearances it now looked a pretty tame and inoffensive looking place.

Mr Ghoulish announced loudly: "And here we are, ladies and gentleman, our piece de resistance! Fifty Berkeley Square – without doubt the most haunted house, not only in London, but possibly the whole of the United Kingdom – and may be the world! Who knows?" There was a series of ah's, from the crowd. "We shall be stopping here for a little while, and the owner has kindly said that we may look around the store for those that wish to do so. And, as a side note, I shall be signing copies of my latest book: Ghouls and Ghosts of Old London Town."

"This is getting so exciting!" said Edie, hardly able to control her excitement. Clive, for his part, was looking even more glum than ever and merely harrumphed once or twice.

"Yes, I'm almost beside myself with anticipation." lied the Devil, placing a hand over his mouth and doing his best to conceal a yawn.

Mr Ghoulish told everyone to stay together, and if by chance anyone spotted anything remotely by way of being supernatural, they were to inform him immediately. By all accounts, only yesterday, he had been rightly informed, that a staff member had witnessed a book falling from a shelf.

"Do you think that we'll see anything?" Edie asked in hopeful anticipation.

"Hope springs eternal," replied the Devil, trying not to sound as bored as he felt. "Hope, definitely, springs eternal."

After the well scripted introduction given by Mr Ghoulish, which included a litany of tales like how George Canning (a former prime minister) had been one of the first to spot some decidedly odd goings on in the house, and how a Captain Kentfield had spent a night in one of the rooms upstairs, only to be found dead the following morning, his face a paroxysm of pure terror, his lips curled back over his gums (pure hokum according to the Devil).

Upon entering the building, the Devil made sure that he was the last to cross the threshold. This was intentional, and owed nothing to being scared of whatever visitations they might encounter. The crowd began to filter inside, one by one, and then disappeared down a corridor. He, on the other hand, moved towards a staircase that had been cordoned off. A small, white plastic chain, carried a sign that read 'STAFF ONLY'. He promptly ignored it and moved silently up the stairs. Turning at the top of the landing, he entered a room situated slightly to the left. It turned out to be a large spacious room, that looked as if it were used purely for storage. There were numerous cardboard boxes piled up at the one end, along with a small wooden table and three chairs. Everything within the room was unnaturally quiet – nothing stirred. Not even the sound of the traffic outside in the street could be heard. All was as quiet as the grave.

Removing his gloves, the Devil sat on a chair and proceeded to wait. There was nothing about the room that gave any indication that there was anything amiss. In fact, the only sound that could be detected was the sound of the occasional timber as it creaked, almost as if the building appeared to breathing peacefully.

He waited patiently. Knowing fully what to expect, his eyes focussed narrowly upon one particular section of the wainscoting, right by the fireplace. After a few minutes of stillness went by, a brown mist began to coalesce at the very self-same spot where the Devil had directed his attention only a short while earlier. Immediately, at the same time this occurred, the temperature in the room began to become icy cold, and a strange unease fell across the entire chamber. It was dark, imposing and without question malevolent. Edie would have loved it, though he doubted that Mr Ghoulish would have. The Devil absolutely did not love it. He had little doubt that many mortals would, by now, be climbing the walls frantically, whilst trying to get out of the room, had they witnessed it.

But then, the Devil was no mere mortal.

As he continued to watch that part of the room, the brown mist began to hover, forever changing its shape, its size fluctuating, getting ever bigger and more menacing by the second. It moved purposely, its form becoming like a huge maw, open wide, black, bottomless and utterly terrifying. This was quickly followed by a series of long sinuous tentacles, endlessly writhing, all with malignant intent. The Devil watched it with sneering contempt and nothing short of amusement.

"Pathetic," he announced, loudly, causing the odd form to stop its cavorting, almost as if it had heard his comment and was utterly bewildered by it. Then it seemed to focus in upon him, as though it were seeing him for who he really was. The nebulous structure then twitched and shuddered violently. This was quickly followed by the sound of an altogether ghostlike voice:

"Oh lummee, it's him!" came a horrified exclamation. At once the brown mist disappeared back into the wainscoting, and the room returned to normal, once again: bright, cheerful and chill free.

Rising slowly from his chair, the Devil walked across to the very spot where the mist had disappeared and then rapped upon the wall loudly with his fist.

"Come out, at once!" he called. The silence remained unbroken. The Devil rapped again. "I strongly suggest that you don't make me come in there and get you! I can assure you if I am obliged to do so you won't like it!"

Slowly, and with great reluctance, an entity appeared from out of the wainscoting. Gone was the imposing haze, the tentacles, the near gut-wrenching fear that had only just now accompanied it – and in its place there stood an altogether diminutive spirit form, its ghostly eyes averted downwards, as if not daring to look directly at their accuser. It stood quietly, swathed in an atmosphere of guilt and shame. The Devil returned to the wall and called out, once again:

"And you! And be quick about it!"

With as near as much hesitancy as the first, a second spirit then emerged; it too seemed altogether ashamed of itself, and stood side by side with the first; where the pair of them then moved self-consciously in fear of what was to come. It all made for a most unusual scene.

The Devil waited for one of them to speak. When after a moment neither of them did so, he asked aggressively:

"Well?"

The first spirit raised itself slightly, and most awkwardly, but without meeting his gaze directly, a gaze that was now searing both of them like an angry furnace.

"Well, what?" it asked timidly, causing the Devil's eyebrows to narrow alarmingly, which was never a good sign.

"I advise you not to try and get smart with me," he warned. "There have been those, a lot greater than you, that have endeavoured to do so – and none of them have succeeded in it. Beware."

"We're sorry," said the second spirit, sounding most uncomfortable, and having said its piece moved back apace.

"Oh, are you, indeed?" said the Devil, not sounding in the least bit convinced by the apology.

"Yes, we didn't mean it," added the first spirit.

"No, we really didn't." followed up the second, just for good measure.

The Devil looked them both up and down. By his expression, it was only too obvious that he didn't like what he saw.

"You didn't mean it?" he repeated. "Frightening honest folk, who are merely going about their daily business - to death in some cases, and you 'didn't mean it?' Well, that makes it all right then, doesn't it? I may as well be off and leave you both to it, so you can continue in much the same vein."

"Oh good. Can we go then?" asked the first spirit, now sounding decidedly brighter in its outlook.

"No, you damn well can't!" barked the Devil in response. "There's to be reparation for what the pair of you have done here, so don't think otherwise!"

The two spirits started alarmingly and then conferred silently to one another. After a moment the first then offered.

"But it's what ghosts do. Frighten people, I mean."

And the second quickly added.

"Yes, and we're earthbound; so, you shouldn't forget that. And it's always expected of ghosts, isn't it, scaring people, that is? Always has been. It's a golden rule, isn't it? So, we aren't really to blame, not if you think about, at least not in that way."

They made it sound as though it was the most natural thing in the world, scaring people to death; and more to the point, that they were the innocent parties in all this and should be better understood, instead of being castigated like as they were.

The Devil's eyebrows had not ceased for a second in their attempt to make contact above his nose, making the two spirits quickly realize that they may just have said the wrong thing. They both looked downwards again most abruptly and went quiet.

"Let me correct you upon one or two points," said the Devil, "Points upon which you both appear to have stored away, somewhere at the back of your understanding. Frightening people to death, by assuming demonic forms, is the work of mindless adolescents with nothing better to do! And because of it, I've a good mind to commit the pair of you to the deepest part of the extremity for your crimes – and what's more you'd both deserve it, too."

Both spirits suddenly became very servile and grovelling in the extreme, and prostrated themselves before him.

"P - Please don't send us there, sir!" begged the first. "We won't do it again! We are truly remorseful, honestly, we are."

"Yes, yes, we are!" added the second. "And we promise not to scare anyone to death, ever again. Please don't send us to Hell! Oh, please don't! Not the abyss, master Devil, sir!"

The Devil raised a hand to silence the two.

"Enough of this damn pettifogging, I say! I have no intention of sending you to Hell. Though it is my intention to banish the pair of you to purgatory for what you have done here. And I want you to realise just how lightly you have gotten off. You can both remain there and kick your heels for a while; and during the course of your banishment, you can reflect upon the error of your ways – let's say for a generation or two. After that we shall speak again on the matter."

"A hundred years?! But that's an eternity!" wailed the first spirit.

"Not quite," corrected the Devil. "Let me ask you a simple question, how long exactly have the pair of you been haunting this establishment?"

The two conferred again.

"For approximately two hundred years, now, sir," answered the second. "But he was here before me, so he's really more responsible, than I am."

"Exactly," responded the Devil. "Then a miserly one hundred years for both of you will be nothing more than a walk in the park now, won't it?"

The first spirit was about to emphasise, that as they were both tied to the property and were unable to leave it, a walk in the park was not really an option for them, despite the fact that it sounded like a nice thing to do. Not wishing to discuss the matter any further, the Devil merely waved his hand and the pair of them suddenly vanished, almost as though they had never been. Their banishment had begun.

Having now returned downstairs, he could see that the rest of the group were all milling around inside the bookshop. As foretold earlier by their host, Mr Ghoulish, he was now busily engaged in signing copies of his latest book; and seemed to be doing it with a relish born of the sound of a cash register ringing loudly in his ears. He sat at a small table, knee deep in his books, applying his signature to anyone willing to part with the worldly sum of twenty-five pounds, which is what it cost to purchase one. As soon as Edie spotted the Devil, she came across to where he stood, eagerly waving her new acquisition.

"Look what I've managed to get," she said, holding up one of the same. The Devil looked closely at it and saw that the front cover was as garish as the leaflet he had obtained from earlier. The front cover was coloured a bright dazzling purple and contained a close-up photograph of the author – make up, costume and all. It looked absolutely ghastly; but judging by the amount of those amongst the group who now were in possession of a copy, he felt that he may have been in the minority in that opinion.

"Well, you are most fortunate," he said to Edie. "I feel sure it will provide you with plenty of night reading, good or otherwise."

"And it was only twenty-five pounds, including the discount. Wasn't that a bargain? And look, he's signed it for me, too." She held it up proudly for him to see.

"A snip at half the price," returned the Devil with a smile, and taking her copy, began to flick through it, though with disguised but obvious distaste. As he was doing this, he stopped at one particular chapter. Looking thoughtfully at it, he then returned the book. "If you will excuse me for just one minute, only I must have a brief word with our tour guide. It's of the most utmost importance."

And, so saying, he made his way through the crowd to where Mr Ghoulish was sitting, signing copies of his book, almost as if they were going out of fashion. As the Devil approached him, he asked brightly: "Would you like me to sign a copy of my book for you?"

"Ah, no, I think not," replied the Devil. "I have a rather weak constitution, and I fear its contents would play havoc with my sleeping arrangements. I merely wished to offer a small piece of advice, that is, if I may be so bold."

"Oh, and what is that?" asked the author.

"If there is ever a reprint in the foreseeable future, and I sincerely hope there is one, be sure that you take out chapter six, as it is a trifle redundant now."

And without further ado, he turned and left the shop, leaving Mr Ghoulish to ponder over precisely what he meant by it.

After word

The rest of the tour continued in much the same vain, minus, the Devil, of course. Having fulfilled his purpose in ridding Berkely Square of all malevolent manifestations, and having more than his fill of Mr Ghoulish, he silently slipped away, leaving Edie and Clive to enjoy the rest of their day; which, by all accounts, at least one of them did.

Nemesis

Being the 19th December – p.m.

Strolling along Oxford Street at an altogether leisurely pace, the Devil allowed himself time in order to take in the splendour of all the Christmas lights that were festooned from one side of the street to the other: there were red, gold, green and blue, all twinkling merrily, splendidly bringing out the festive enchantment that only became present once a year. He did so love it. It was the one time of the year when real magic actually materialised on earth; it filled the air, and became manifest amongst mankind; causing at least some of them to be a little kinder and a little more charitable towards their fellow man. Of course, it went without saying, that there would always be the die-hards, those whose hearts were shut up solid, like a fortress, those for whom Christmas cheer and compassion meant little more than an ideal opportunity to take advantage of others. It was people such as this that he now targeted. Not that rooting out such low-life's gave him any satisfaction. It didn't. It wasn't as if he got any gratuitous pleasure out of it, no, the bottom line was it was his job, and as the old idiom went – 'someone had to do it'. People, well at least some of them, were often obliged to be shown how to learn a lesson. And those that chose not to learn a lesson, or two? Well, there was always an alternative – and plan B rarely failed to suffice.

He watched the people hurrying by, scurrying back and forth, and looking for all the world as if someone had previously filmed them, and was then running it back again, only this time with the speed increased. Christmas had a habit of doing this. Seasonal shopping and the last-minute gifts – gifts that, in all probability, the recipients rarely wanted – or even retained after the Christmas period had passed. But it kept the world turning year after year, and the smiles on the peoples faces, whether genuine or not, only ever added to the festive good humour, and so the magic proliferated. And it was wonderful, regardless.

My - my, the Devil thought to himself as he passed the shops, witnessing all the new-fangled technologies that were currently up for sale: there were phones, games, computers and a myriad of other things, things that only spoke to him of mystery and confusion and a strong desire not to get involved. Traditional ways were becoming a thing of the past, but then the very passing of time did just that. Everything changed, and not all of it for the good. A very unpleasant thought then crossed his mind – was everything slowly passing him by? Was that at all possible for him? No, surely not. Silly thought. He was, after all, the Devil, wasn't he? That alone gave him a modicum of standing in the world, a certain kudos if you will. He stood gazing at his reflection in a shop window, and was shocked to see something he hadn't noticed before. Was that a touch of grey at his temples – and was that a small wrinkle to the left of his right eye? He shook himself and instantly looked a hundred years younger. Not that any of the passers-by noticed. But he did, and it caused him a wry smile. The old magic was still there. You just had to dig it out every once in a while.

Taking out his pocket watch and note-book, he consulted both. The watch showed the time to be 4.47p.m., which meant he still had a few minutes in which to get to his next rendezvous. He replaced the watch and flicked through the note-book. A single name was written at the top of the page. It read Nobby Bracknell. Why was it, he wondered, that all petty criminals and thieves known to him always had a name that seemed to reflect their profession? It made little or no sense to him at all. He replaced the note-book and waited, choosing to secrete himself within the shop doorway of a large colourful boutique, ensuring that he was well out of the way of shoppers.

After a few minutes spent idly watching the world go by, wishing people the compliments of the season and just generally killing time, his eye alighted upon a young man who was walking along the street, seemingly minding his own business. He was quite short, wiry and looked in his early twenties. He also had a black cap pulled down, which covered most of his face. The Devil decided that this looked positively questionable, and for a very good reason too. As he continued to watch the young man, he entered a large exclusive department store. The Devil followed at a distance and at a leisurely pace.

Nobby appeared to move with a singular purpose, milling amongst the shoppers of the crowded store, occasionally bumping into buyers, apologising profusely and then moving on once again. As the Devil continued to watch and follow on from behind, he noted that Nobby's tastes were now apparently changing, becoming somewhat more lavish. The young man had now moved on to the jewellery department on the first floor, where he pretended to browse in an almost nonchalant, laid-back manner. Having caught the attention of the sales assistant's eye, he then asked to view numerous items; those being rings, watches and a host of other very expensive items. This continued for some time, with Nobby apparently changing his mind on so many occasions, requesting more items to view, that the poor assistant was becoming so weighed down with confusion it was near impossible to keep track of everything that had been laid out to view. After what appeared to be much dithering, deliberation and prevarication, the young man could be heard expressing his doubt as to whether anything he had seen was precisely what he was looking for, as he wanted a particular Christmas gift. Thanking the assistant, he then turned and left, saying he would think things over and possibly return later once he had finally made up his mind.

At this point the Devil decided that now was a perfectly good moment to reel the lad in. So, advancing on him from the rear, he placed a firm hand upon his shoulder and gave it a gentle squeeze.

"Nobby!" he announced with undisguised glee, as if he were greeting an old friend who he hadn't seen for some considerable time.

Realizing at once that the game was up and that he had been rumbled, and also not recognizing the man who had addressed him as anyone he knew, Nobby did what he always did in situations like this – he bolted. Twisting out of the Devil's grasp, with as much dexterity as a greased weasel, he ran straight out of the store and on into the coming traffic, dodging this way and that, until he was quickly out of sight. The Devil watched him go, not in the least concerned by it all.

"Fast little bunny rabbit, aren't you?" he muttered to himself, and slowly began to saunter in the same direction after the young man, as though he had all the time in the world. Which, being the Devil, he did.

Nobby was used to making good his escape, and had done so many times previously. It was almost as though it was an integral part of what he did for a living; though it had to be said that it was more of an occupational hazard than anything else. Once he was across Oxford Street, he turned right into Berber Street, then left and then made for a small alleyway he was all too familiar with. After all this effort, he felt convinced that he made good his escape. There wasn't a copper born, or a security guard for that matter, he couldn't out pace. Mind you, it had been a close-run thing there for a moment and it had given him quite a scare. Usually, he was pretty adept at spotting anyone on his tail, be it a copper, or anyone else. Not quite sure how this one had eluded him. The guy must be good, no doubt about it. No matter, it was time he moved onto Leicester Square anyway. There were always rich pickings there at this time of year. The prospect very nearly made his mouth drool.

"Nobby!" came a voice he recognised immediately, which nearly caused him to drop to the floor with apoplexy. The Devil stood before him, grinning from ear to ear. "Nobby Bracknell, well who would have thought it. As I live and breathe! You ran off before we had a chance to introduce ourselves."

Before he had even time to think, instinct once again took over and Nobby was off once more. Running at break neck speed, he shot out of the alleyway and immediately turned left. There was no one born that knew the back alleys and bolt-holes of London like he did. He could outpace this guy any day of the week. And it was this thought that was now central to his thinking, and altogether paramount to his motivation. He ran, turned, turned again and then doubled back, always keeping to the alleyways and side streets. After about ten minutes or so, he slowed slightly and looked to see if he was being pursued. All was clear, and with no sign of the copper anywhere. He sighed heartily and slowed his pace. Time for a breather he reckoned. He calculated that if he stayed put for twenty minutes or so, then the law would give up looking for him and would move on. They always did, and then he could do the same, only he would go down the Tottenham Court Road, then the Charing Cross Road and on into Leicester Square, that way. He had to admit that he would be glad of a few minutes rest; all that running had taken it out of him. Up until a few minutes ago his lungs had felt as if they were on fire.

Then, without any prior warning, the voice came again. It was like a recurring nightmare.

"Nobby," it said, gleefully.

Dear God in heaven! Him again? It just wasn't possible. But it was – it was the same guy, here, again! – and not even out of breath – and seemingly dogging his every step. How the hell did he keep doing it? What was going on here? Nobby went to flee for a third time, only now he found that when he tried to do so he couldn't move, not so much as an inch. Looking down he saw that both of his feet appeared to be encased in what looked like a block of solid concrete. How was that possible? This couldn't be happening! He tried dragging himself, but only succeeded in falling on his backside. The man watched him with apparent amusement, even taking time out to casually unfold a chair he appeared to have brought with him for just this occasion. Sitting on it in front of him, the man finally spoke.

"Fruitless exercise," he said. "And not to mention an utter waste of time and energy on your part, Nobby. Me, I can do this for eternity – not that I need to, of course. Anyhow, you're staying put my lad, that is until I choose otherwise. Just let me know when you are ready to discuss matters sensibly. I'll be here waiting patiently for you."

And saying that he promptly took out a newspaper and begin flicking though its pages. Just who the hell was this guy?

Nobby spent an unproductive few minutes trying to extricate himself from the concrete that held him firm, and found that he couldn't. He only succeeded in exhausting himself further. Eventually he slumped back against the wall, beaten, physically admonished and thoroughly bamboozled by what was happening to him.

Was it all a nightmare that he would suddenly wake up from? It certainly seemed real enough.

"What do you want from me, man?" he finally asked. "And how did you do this trick with my feet?"

The Devil slowly folded his newspaper, allowing it to disappear into the ether and then looked up.

"Glad I have your full attention, at last, Nobby. Just a simple exercise in saving us both a little time and you an awful lot of energy. The adamant around your feet will keep you from even considering flight, or even fight mode. And take it from me, you aren't up to either at the moment."

"Are you the law?" asked a bemused Nobby.

The Devil looked thoughtful.

"Well, I suppose in a manner of speaking, yes I am - in an unofficial capacity, that is," he said. "However, I find it all rather relative at the end of the day. As that old Americanism goes, 'It's all one big crap-chute anyway.' But I digress. Nobby, we need to talk. We really do need to have a con-flab, you and I."

"Look man, I can cut you in, if that's what you want. That's not a problem for me. We can make a deal. I'm up for it. You have my word on that, honest. And now, can you please get his stuff off my feet - it's killing me?"

"No, and no," replied the Devil. "That's not how I work, not at all. You see, I call the shots; I always have and I always will. That's unequivocal. There's no room for negotiation, it's either - or, I'm afraid; cut and dried, black and white. You either do as I tell you – or, you suffer the consequences. In the scheme of things, it's all pretty simple. And it generally works well, I find."

Nobby didn't like the sound of that one bit. It was obvious that he had strayed too far, or this guy was looking to take over his patch. If that happened then he wouldn't be left with a pot to piss in. No, he reckoned he'd go along with whatever he had to say, for now at least, that's if it got him free from this mess. He could always renege on it later. This guy had some weird power and he wasn't at all sure what it was, or how he managed to achieve what he did, but better to pretend to do as he wanted until it suited him to do otherwise.

"Look man, I had no idea I was on your turf, I really didn't. But now I know, you won't see me around here again, that's a promise. Just let me go and I'll be history, you'll see. I'll move on, and that'll be it, honest, I truly mean it."

The Devil sighed and shook his head sadly and said merely one word.

"Hubris."

"Who's that, man?" asked Nobby, failing to follow the Devil's direction. "This Hubris, is he someone else you want me to cut in? That's ok with me. Not a problem."

"The word hubris means dangerous, or over confident, Nobby and it is a long arduous route that you are currently travelling. Let me assure you, this route is very gruelling and steeped in great danger for you. My advice would be, to stop now, consider and turn back while you may. To do anything otherwise would make you later realise what a terrible error you have made."

The Devil's words made little sense to the young man, but if anything, affected him more so on a subconscious level. It was true, he had no idea what the man was going on about, but felt deep within him that things weren't how they should be. Without knowing why, it scared him. Either way he thought it better to try and blag his way out of it.

"I'm being honest with you, man. Cut me some slack and I'm out of here and that's the truth. I'll be gone."

The Devil didn't look unconvinced by the lad's attempt at being sincere.

"Well, Nobby, we can continue with this charade forever and a day, all the while you paying me lip service, but intending to do something else, or you can save us both a lot of time and messing about. It's just a case of initialising what little common sense you were born with, and then fully comprehend the complete hopelessness of your situation. As I said previously, it's either - or. Eternity awaits your pleasure. What's it to be?"

Having his very thoughts viewed and then thrown back at him, hit Nobby like a thunderbolt. His mind became a whirl of unknowns, fears and a thorough inability to comprehend what was going on. It totally besieged his brain, making it difficult to get to grips with what was playing out here.

"Yeah, ok." was all he could think of to say, hoping it would pacify this guy a little, and what's more give him some time to weigh things up further. Needless to say, it didn't.

"A question for you, Nobby," said the Devil. "And a pretty simple one at that. Have you any idea what the term Nemesis means?"

Nobby, feeling utterly confused, shook his head.

"Er, no," he replied.

"Well, in short, my boy, Nemesis refers to someone who dispenses retribution, or inflicts vengeance on those that have committed a crime, of one sort or another. Divine retribution if you like. In some instances, the retribution can be dire and without mercy, but then that will often depend upon the one being subjected to said retribution, and of course upon a genuine willingness to change. Are you keeping up with me?"

"No, not really," admitted Nobby, wondering what on earth the guy was going on about.

"Then let's simplify it for you a little, shall we? As they say, a picture will often paint a thousand words. Now, I suggest that you pay close attention. Your very fate hangs in the balance here. Okay. And off we go."

The Devil pointed to the wall opposite. And, as he did so, it instantly lit up like a film screen. Nobby looked about to see where it was coming from, but there seemed no obvious place to put a projector. As he watched, images suddenly appeared on the screen, hundreds and thousands of them, images of people surrounded by what looked like hideous demons of every sort. The imagery was horrific: boiling blood, fire and brimstone, screams, torment, limbs hacked from bodies, writhing fire, eternal damnation. As he watched, transfixed and unable to avert his gaze, sweat broke out on his forehead, despite the chilly evening. Rivulets of it ran down his back. And although the film he was watching lasted for no more than a minute at most, to Nobby, it could easily have been a decade. When it finally ended, the images slowly faded away, leaving nothing behind but a graffiti covered wall again.

Getting to his feet, the Devil leaned forward, as was his won't, and grinned almost malevolently. It was a grin that spoke of pure unadulterated victory, and nothing less, and he relished in its effect upon his quarry.

"It makes Hieronymus Bosch look a bit tame, don't you think?" he said. "Almost like a walk in the park on a nice summer's afternoon in comparison. And there's something that you need to realise here, Nobby, and that is what you have just witnessed is only the first level of hell. Yes, that is what I said. You may take my word for it, when I tell you, that it gets significantly worse the further down you go. Much worse, in fact. Not a place you're likely to book for your annual hols. You really would not like it one bit. It's most definitely a place to avoid, that is if you have a choice – and you presently do have a choice, Nobby, but you may take my word for it that this choice is disappearing fast."

The memory of what Nobby had witnessed stayed with him, forever etched in his brain, an eternal reminder of things that had no right to be. Pulling himself upright he grabbed the wall for support, feeling that he was about to pass out with the sheer nausea that he was now experiencing. The Devil stood watching him with interest. It was something that he had witnessed many times before during his existence. The outcome was always the same. It never digressed from the norm. And knowing this, he gave Nobby a moment or two to consider his situation, and more importantly, to take on board precisely what he had just observed, before finally commenting.

"Interesting viewing. Though it has to be said, it isn't anything you would want to see ever again. Wouldn't you agree?"

Nobby couldn't respond to the question. It was as if his soul had just been forcibly ripped from his body – exposed to reality and fate in its most brutal and starkest form. The Devil understood only too well the effect the unadorned realization of hell had on people and especially on a human's mental state. And it had to be said, it was never good.

"Are you aware, Nobby, that the name Lucifer, roughly translated, means Light Bringer? You didn't know that? Oh well, an odd designation I think, but one of much poignancy; yes, much poignancy. Well now, I have a little proposition for you. It's nothing too arduous, so don't fret unduly about it. It will simply take a bit of work on your part." Taking an envelope from his pocket, he said. "In here is a list of all the people and stores you have stolen from over the past few weeks. It is now up to you to make reparation. I would heartily recommend an immediate start, if I were you. 'Tomorrow is too late' as the aphorism goes. Handing the envelope to Nobby, he then turned to leave, before finally offering one last piece of advice. "And may I suggest that you pray with the very essence of your being that you never see me again – ever! Believe me, when I say, it wouldn't be an experience that would leave you in any form of rapture or euphoria. Oh, and have a very good Christmas while you're about it. I believe there might be snow later. Fingers crossed and all that."

A very distraught Nobby called after the vanishing figure.

"But what about this concrete on my feet?!!!"

The Devil stopped and turned.

"Concrete? What concrete?" he said and promptly vanished.

After word

The transformation that was brought about in Nobby, through the Devil's intervention, was near instantaneous. To begin with, he insisted on dropping the name Nobby and requested that everyone now call him by his proper Christian name; that being Neville. Everything that he had purloined that day was returned to its rightful owner, be it person or store, which meant in some instances, him having to travel miles in order to fulfil his charge. Any offers of a reward by those he was returning items to was always refused with great courtesy, explaining that he was only too pleased to be able to make good their misfortune. The recipients all thought well of him for it. Another positive outcome of Neville's brief, but impressionable meeting with the Devil, was that he began attending church on a regular basis. This extended to helping to pass the plate at the end of each service and exhorting those in the congregation to give – give – give, not only for the good of their souls, but also for their own personal deliverance in this life. For the rest of his days, he never ever encountered the Devil again, but he always ensured that he was always indoors before darkness fell. And he always made a point of never going to Oxford Street, not ever, Christmas or no. His days of deleterious activities were truly at an end.

The See-er in the Dark

Being the 20ᵗʰ December – a.m.

It hadn't snowed the previous evening, nor had it snowed at any time throughout the morning; there was not so much as a single flake of the stuff. The Devil felt altogether peeved because of it. No snow. It piqued him; more so than he cared to let on. He wasn't the sort of individual that spoke of snow in condescending terms, as many so often did. 'Oh, I personally think it looks lovely on a Christmas card, though I can't abide the stuff in reality. Far too cold and unpleasant.' Well, he could. It was truly glorious stuff. For him it was the very quintessential essence of Christmas, and there was nothing more splendid than walking out onto a fresh bed of the stuff, in very large boots. It was like stepping onto freshly crumbed meringue, that someone had purposefully sprinkled on the ground, specifically for that very purpose. There was nothing better.

He surveyed the cloudless sky. There was not a hint of grey to be seen anywhere. Voicing an undecipherable expletive beneath his breath; he slowly moved on. There was plenty to do, snow or no snow.

As he was running slightly ahead of schedule that morning, he chose to take a morning constitutional along the south bank. It was always a walk that he enjoyed, and had done for a good many centuries. He spent some time taking in the expansive view of the river Thames, and gave some thought to how much it had changed down the years. Far more bridges now for one thing. Way back then you had a multitude of small boats, all ferrying people and goods back and forth, all day every day. His mind went back to the old London Bridge, the second one to be more precise, the one that had been constructed in 1209. Now that was a bridge! It was definitely on a par with one of these new-fangled shopping centres, he thought; and contained virtually everything a person could want: ale houses, a bakery, chop houses – why it even had a church! But when all was said and done, it was pretty narrow, now he came to think about it; its width being only broad enough to allow a single horse and cart to pass at any one time, in any direction. Not practical at all really, and certainly no good if you were in a rush. And naturally, it stank; stank something awful, but then so did the entire population of London, including both the ne'er do wells and the rich. The stench was something frightful, if he was honest. Much better nowadays. Most present-day people paid far greater attention to personal hygiene than they did back then. Well, at least the majority of people did. Not all, admittedly.

Sitting outside a café, he ordered himself a black coffee and a slice of rich fruit cake. Decadent in the extreme –

but who cared, it was nearly Christmas, and he deserved it, didn't he? It would be unlikely that he would be brought to task over it. To hell with it, he thought, and what's more he meant it.

Despite there being a decided nip in the air, he wasn't at all bothered by it. In fact, the colder the better as far as he was concerned. It merely made for a very pleasant change from the heat. A pigeon flew down unexpectedly and landed on the rim of the chair directly opposite to where he was sitting. It showed a distinct lack of perspicacity in doing so and cast an altogether covetous eye on his remaining piece of cake. Looking up, it caught the Devil's burning, baleful gaze simmering at just a few feet distant and at once squawked loudly and fell off the chair, where it landed with a resounding thud. Slowly and indeed most unsteadily, it got to its feet and began to drag itself away in the opposite direction to where the Devil was seated. It didn't really care where it was headed, but anywhere was preferable to here. The Devil watched it go, and then took immediate pleasure in finishing off the rest of the cake, crumbs and all. It verged on the wicked; but he could live with it.

After paying the bill, the Devil took a napkin and wiped any specks from his mouth and beard, and then taking out a small mirror checked his reflection. His appearance looked altogether fine and thoroughly met with his approval.

Satisfied that all was well, he continued with his morning constitutional.

One thing that did occur to him as he walked, and that was, irrespective of how many times he wished the odd passer-by a very good morning that day, few rarely ever responded in kind. If anything, he only ever received some very queer looks. People were definitely becoming more insular and less gregarious, he thought to himself. The ever-changing face of the world in which they lived.

Sauntering, and without any thought of undue hurry, he stopped every now and then so as to take in his surroundings. At one point he came across a bookseller displaying a large stock of various tomes, mainly paper-backs, all laid out upon numerous trestle tables. Everything was in alphabetical order, which made perusal that much easier. After spending some time viewing what was on offer, his eye alighted upon one particular book that read 'The Devil Rides Out'. Most odd, he thought, it doesn't specify as to where I am supposed to have ridden out from, and, more to the point, upon what and where to. He hastily replaced it, muttering 'garbage' beneath his breath as he did so.

Some-time later, another would be customer picked up the very same book, and failed to understand how the stall holder could ask the costly sum of £6.00 for a second-hand paperback, that was so severely scorched, both for and aft. It really was daylight robbery nowadays.

After much tardiness, the Devil finally arrived at the day's first port of call. The Globe theatre on the south bank. As he stood before the replica of Shakespeare's original, this being his first viewing of it, he cast a critical eye over it, and it had to be said he found nothing but praise for the structure. Naturally, it went without saying that it couldn't hold a candle to the original, though that was hardly surprising. A tour guide approached him; no doubt eager for a potential sale.

"Did you know," she said, chirpily, "that the original Globe theatre was situated on the other side of the water in the east end of London? Very few people are aware of that."

The Devil smiled broadly.

"Yes, I did as a matter of fact. And if it wasn't for my suggestion at the time, of taking the whole thing down, lock stock and barrel I may add, and moving it to here, then you wouldn't be standing there now talking to me about it. We managed to do it all in one night, can you believe, though it has to be said, the original edifice was placed a little further way over to the left, there."

The young woman looked at him completely askance, gave an awkward smile, and then hurriedly moved on. A definite nut-case, if ever there was one.

Curtness, was generally not included in the Devil's repertoire, he usually had little or no time for it. But he thought he had handled it pretty well, everything taken into consideration. He, not wanting a lengthy discourse on the Globe theatre, or its origins, chose to let her down gently. It had ultimately achieved the desired result.

At last, he found a suitable bench upon which to sit, which enabled him to have a good view of the entrance to the theatre. So, sitting, and getting himself relatively comfortable, he went through his daily routine of consulting his pocket watch and notebook. There were still a few minutes to go before the person he was waiting for showed up. Going through the pages of the notebook, he stopped at a particular page and ran his finger down the entries, and then stopped.

"Ah, here we are," he said, satisfied. "Albert Cambledon-Brown. Aged 46. Charlatan and thief…" He continued to read through the entry, pursing his lips disapprovingly as he did so. Once finished, his opinion of Mr Cambledon-Brown had slumped alarmingly. This did not augur well for the gentleman in any way. "My oh my. I see we have one here that is bad to the very bone. I think perhaps a little corrective therapy is in order. Ah, and if I am not very much mistaken, here comes our Mr Cambledon-Brown now. By the pricking of my thumbs, something wicked this way comes."

As he sat watching, a short rotund individual hove into view. The man was wearing a threadbare tweed suit, that looked as though it had seen numerous better days, but was worn undoubtedly for the effect it gave, one of penury. There was something about him that the Devil initially found difficult to quantify, something about the way he walked and moved and edged his way into position outside the theatre. It had nothing to do with the white cane and small dark spectacles, obviously intended to fool the public, but something definitely more. The façade did not fool him one bit. He thought that it was like watching a snake, as it slowly eased itself inch by inch, and bit by bit into a secretive niche, where it could easily ambush its prey. The whole scenario was decidedly creepy.

The man set up a large cap in front of where he stood, along with a sign, which read: BLIND AND HOMELESS. EX ARMY VETERAN. PENNILESS –

EVICTED – FORGOTTEN BY THOSE HE
FOUGHT FOR. PLEASE GIVE GENEROUSLY.
Well, there was nothing like laying it on thick, was there?

Virtually within moments of his arrival, money began
flowing freely into the cap. At each separate instance
there was a muted 'Much obliged' from Albert, or a
'Thank you so much.' It even sounded genuine, which
irritated the Devil even more.

And, so the morning wore on. If at any time he felt that
his sign was beginning to lose any indication of impact,
Albert began to moan a little as if in obvious pain, or he
would drop his white cane – and then make a great show
of trying to locate it again. He even called out plaintively
at one point 'Help a poor unfortunate that has fallen
upon hard times!' By lunch time he had amassed more
money that the majority of people usually made in three
days of honest work; though he made a great point of
emptying his cap each time it showed any sign of looking
too full.

The Devil continued to watch him, with an admixture of
growing fascination and utter loathing for the man. After
studying an elderly woman, who hardly looked as if she
could afford it, deposit a five-pound note in his hat, he
heard himself mutter, 'Insidious little worm!' Things
were beginning to look decidedly unhealthy for Albert.

And, so the charade continued unabated, Albert
continuing to milk the hapless public of everything he
could, and the Devil continuing to watch him. By mid-
afternoon, his pockets were now so swollen with ill-
gotten gains, he decided that he had had enough for the
day. Slowly, he began to collect his few items together

and then moved off. It was difficult not to notice that his face now carried a certain smugness about it. This also got under the Devil's skin, and he felt obliged to make a note about it in his book.

Ensuring that he didn't get too close, the Devil tagged along a short way behind, giving the impression that he was simply someone out for a stroll. After covering less that two hundred yards from where he had been begging outside the Globe theatre, Albert quickly lost the dark spectacles. The white cane was summarily folded away and pocketed, leaving him to go on his merry way, whole again and without a disability in sight. Obviously feeling the need, he then entered a riverside bar and ordered himself a, what he chose to call, a well-earned drink. After all, it was thirsty work conning the public. The Devil sat opposite him and ordered himself a tonic water, continuing to watch Albert's every move. He couldn't help but notice that every so often his left hand strayed to his jacket pocket, as he felt the fruits of his labours, the pocket veritably bulging with the menial efforts of his underhanded ways.

Albert ordered a second drink, and when this was quaffed, he then ordered a third; all the while the Devil sat patiently, watching him closely, biding his time. After feeling that he was now suitably well oiled, but not sufficiently too far gone to drive home, he left the bar.

"Our venal friend, with his venal ways, is on the move," muttered the Devil and followed him out of the bar.

Albert was feeling pretty good about himself. It never ceased to amaze him just how gullible folk could be. Total suckers the lot of them. A white stick, a pair of dark glasses and a sign professing destitution. And they lapped it up. He patted his pocket once again and felt happy and totally replete. Life was good, and he was laughing all the way to the bank. When he felt in this state of mind, he knew that nothing could faze him. He felt altogether blessed. Little did he know that his negative and somewhat unethical behaviour was about to result in negative consequences of the gravest kind, and that they were literally just around the corner. Justice was about to come a-calling.

As he made his way down Clink Street and the site of the ill-famed debtors-prison; he had no inkling that he was being followed, or of what was to come; then why should he? The Devil looked about and remarked how everything had been significantly spruced up since he had been here last; then increased his pace somewhat, not wishing to lose sight of his target. A short time later he saw Albert pass Tower Bridge and make for a small side turning. Once there, he approached a very nice, sleek looking vehicle. Opening the drivers-door, he climbed in. Then placing the keys in the ignition, he turned the key and waited for the engine to fire. Nothing happened. He tried again. The result was the same. He tried a third time. Still nothing. He was now of the opinion that the battery was probably flat. But it shouldn't be, as the car was virtually new. Probably an electrical fault or some such. There was always something.

"Panoramic views, don't you think? Of the river, I mean." came a voice next to him, the shock of which nearly caused Albert to asphyxiate on the spot.

"What the f-!" he exclaimed, and turning, saw a well-dressed man sitting next to him in the passenger seat, not knowing how he had got there. "Who the hell are you? And how did you get in here?" he demanded to know.

It was common knowledge, by those that knew him, that the Devil had a particularly wry sense of humour. And it was also known by those he regularly imposed it upon, to attest to the same. This instance was to prove no exception. Taking out a small business card, the Devil handed it across. Albert took it and examined it carefully, before crying out angrily:

"There's nothing on it! It's blank!"

Leaning closer, the Devil whispered in his ear, "I'm incognito."

"Get out of my car!" Albert roared, believing wholeheartedly that an aggressive approach would serve him best, as the man was clearly a lunatic and would respond to nothing less. Best to go on the offensive. He was of course completely wrong in this assumption.

"I will do no such thing," replied the Devil, intentionally sounding rather petulant. "And what's more, you can't make me."

Feeling that he had given this lunatic enough opportunity to get out of his car, and now also detecting a hint of belligerence in the man's tone, Albert reached down and grabbed a small wooden club from the side of his seat, a club made of good old English Oak, a solid club that would be the perfect tool to stove this man's head in, if push came to shove. And he'd do it, too.

The Devil smiled benignly.

"The weather is altogether clement, considering the time of year, that is, don't you think? Let's go for a walk, Albert, just the two of us. I'm sure it will be educational."

Albert brandished the club in a very threatening way.

"I'm damned if I will!" he shouted. "Now get out of this car before I part your hair with this!"

"Oh, dear – dear – dear," said the Devil. "You know, I am reminded of an old expression: 'Not enough room in which to swing a cat'. I believe the saying is rather apt at present. What do you think? The question was rhetorical, by the way and doesn't need a response."

Looking down, Albert could see that the wooden club had somehow miraculously transformed itself into a fluffy toy pink cat. Instantly he dropped it, as if it were red hot and would burn him.

The Devil continued to smile and as he did so he gave Albert's arm a gentle squeeze.

"The offer of a walk wasn't a request," he said, with great poignancy, and promptly got out of the car.

A strange sensation then began to spread itself over Albert. It started across his shoulders and extended rapidly throughout the rest of his anatomy. Along with this odd sensation, he also felt as if his will had been utterly removed from his control. He had no desire to go for a walk with this man, and normally nothing on earth would have induced him to do so; that is, in normal circumstances. But these were not normal circumstances any longer - he had now become a thrall of the very Devil. Feeling unable to prevent himself from doing so, he got out of the car and followed meekly behind the stranger, who now appeared to be holding a cane, and a rather dapper one at that.

The Devil set off along the Thames in a westerly direction, swinging his cane merrily as he went. Albert followed along like a dependable pet, dogging his steps faithfully, but not having any idea as to why he was doing so.

They continued walking until they came to Blackfriars Bridge, and then the Devil stopped. Looking up at the steel girders beneath, he casually pointed at them with his cane.

"Are you aware, Albert, that a few years ago, an Italian banker was found hanging from just up there? Just there to the left. Roberto Calvi was his name. No-one was quite sure whether it was murder, or suicide. He worked for the Vatican, you see, and was known as 'God's banker'. Of course, it goes without saying that if God was one of his client's, then the Almighty must have turned a bit of a blind eye on the day he died, or so it seems. Perhaps he wasn't happy with the level of service he was receiving. Charges too high? Insufficient over-draft facilities, or some such? What's your opinion?"

"Er – I don't have one." Albert heard himself mutter. And he didn't. Nothing seemed to make any sense to him at all. What was he doing here with this man?

"No, of course you don't, and why should you? It was just a thought. Not at all important, I'm sure. No more than a brief aside. Let's move on, shall we?"

As they continued with their walk, Albert was finding it rather difficult to come to terms with his inability to merely go off in the other direction in which he was currently travelling. He certainly wanted to. Every sinew and fibre of his being told him this. But he couldn't achieve that desire, not if his very life depended on it. His will was powerless. None existent in fact.

"You may know, or not know," said the Devil indicating the river. "That the police on the Thames here are the oldest police force in the world? Yes, hard to believe, I know, but it's true nevertheless. And they actually pre-date the Metropolitan Police by about thirty years or so. Utterly fascinating, don't you think?"

Albert nodded. Though he didn't care one way or another; all he wanted to do was to go home. If only his feet would obey him. The Devil, sensing his unease, moved a little closer and placed an arm about his shoulder, in an altogether comforting manner. Though it did little to dispel Albert's feeling of unease.

"We need to digress a little now, Albert. And what I mean by this is, we have to touch upon the essence of why we are actually here. It requires us to be a bit more, how shall we say, a little more serious about matters. There's an important issue that we need to discuss at length. And it's my duty to inform you that it's an issue that may well determine the very outcome of your whole future existence. Do you comprehend what I am saying to you?"

"Yes," he replied. "Yes, I do."

Needless to say, Albert hadn't the foggiest notion what the man was going on about, and was equally convinced that the man had somehow drugged him without him being aware of it, hence the constant acquiescence on his part. He'd heard about drugs that could do that sort of thing when administered. Nothing else made any sense.

The Devil smiled, as he was often wont to do in circumstances such as this. Things were going well, he thought.

"That's good to know, Albert. It should make my purpose in being here that much easier. Now, I have a question for you. It's nothing too difficult. But give it some thought. Have you any idea what a Crawler is? Is it a term you have ever come across before?" Albert answered in the negative. "No? Then let us sit upon this bench for a while and I shall do my utmost to enlighten you." And, so they sat, Albert desperately wondering as to what might possibly be coming next. The Devil smiled. "There, that's better. Now, as I was saying, the expression Crawler; it was a term used to refer to a certain class of people who lived - though a better and more precise term would have been existed – and they resided on these very streets, approximately one hundred and fifty years ago. They were, in the main, so destitute and in a state of such intense impoverishment, they actually accosted beggars for hand-outs. Give that some thought for a moment. Accosting a beggar for a handout. Can you actually believe that? Absolutely mind-boggling, I think. Horrendous thought. A really terrible state of affairs to be in. Well, I want you to dwell on that fact for a moment or two longer. Think about what it actually meant for these poor people. Consider, if you will, what life must have been like for these poor unfortunates, born to a life of such intense low degradation that the majority of the populace didn't even regard them as being human. Utterly horrifying, don't you know?"

Albert thought about it, and agreed that life must have been pretty bleak for them. The Devil then asked him to endeavour to put himself, if he could, in their position. Albert gave the semblance of doing so, but found it difficult to relate to how these people must have lived, so very long ago in the way that they did. Life was different now, things were different, everything had moved on.

The Devil watched him closely, gauging his response, reading his very thoughts and seeing how his own words had impacted upon his soul. After a few moments of contemplation, it became evident to him that Albert just wasn't getting it. He wasn't making that all important connection which would have altered his very way of life and more importantly his overall view on those around him; being his fellow man. More stringent methods were required, he thought.

"I firmly believe, Albert, that the severity of the situation calls for a more intimate experience, in order to fully enable you to earn a greater understanding of what I am getting at here," he said.

This revelation caused Albert a certain amount of consternation and unease. Despite not being subjected to anything remotely approaching mental anguish, or physical hurt during his time with this stranger, something deep within the confines of his being told him that this was all about to change. And he was not wrong in that assumption, either. He quickly became aware that his personal world was now changing, and changing swiftly, and what's more, radically, too. The skyline became dark, sombre and menacing; everything around him, buildings, people; the entire vista that now filled his vision took on a grey graveness that seared his very soul. It was terrifying to behold. His world looked like a waking nightmare, surrounded by soot blackened houses, set against a similar skyline. There was no colour to be seen anywhere. The air was acrid, filthy and unbreathable and he could actually taste it. People, if the term could rightly be applied to them, scurried in an altogether languid, unhurried fashion, weighed down by the existence fate had decreed for them. No light shone beyond the blank gaze of those that existed in this place. To all intents and purpose, they were soulless, lacking any human feelings and qualities, devoid of any characteristic that would have shown them to be human.

As Albert watched them, a dank coldness seemed to grip his very soul, it seemed to strangle and smother it, until he felt as though he was now unable to breath. The people he saw about him all moved with a single purpose, trying to escape the freezing cold wind and the driving rain, shifting from doorway to doorway, ingress to ingress, anywhere that might offer some slight modicum of shelter; though it was only too apparent that it rarely did. Women, clutched small children, and even babies, wrapping what clothes or shawls they possessed around their shoulders, as they tried to keep warm. The overriding sensation was one of sheer and complete hopelessness; no salvation was evident and none was forthcoming. This was sheer hell on earth and personified everything that the Devil was supposed to endorse. The people here were driven by a despair so deep and profound it appeared to caress their very souls – and yes, souls they had, souls that cried out for compassion. But these were the forgotten people, those that no-one wanted, and society at large had no time for. England had an empire, but these unfortunates were not a part of it.

"Dear God!" exclaimed Albert in utter horror. "What is this place and who are these people?"

"Why Albert, these people are you. Every single last one of them. You are both one and the same," replied the Devil. "You have so much in common, it surprises me that you cannot see it. Look again. Look closer!"

"These people are me?" he cried in horror, knowing that what he has hearing was true, but not daring to ask how or why it could be possible.

The Devil looked upon him dispassionately.

"Different time, same venue, Albert. You seem altogether shocked. These people you see before you are the Crawlers I spoke of not so very long ago. They represent the lowest rank of people on the social scale – they are the hoi polloi, if you like – the rank and file – the commonality. These are the people that society does not want, does not recognize, they are the unseen masses. These are the unreal. They possess nothing but the wretchedness that envelopes their very existence in this realm. Why, they don't even have the energy with which to beg. What you see here is the inevitable consequence of the human condition, when compassion is no longer present. And this is what fate has in store for you, Albert – that is, unless you choose to change your ways. And believe me, fate is never left cheated. Not ever. You see, reincarnation is not linear, as you might imagine. You may just as easily end up here as one of these poor wretches as anywhere else in time. It all depends upon what lesson you need to learn. The writing is on the wall for you my friend, and it is etched in utter misery. You are advised to take great heed."

Albert looked on in helpless terror, fearing what he saw, but more so fearing what the stranger had revealed to him of his own possible fate. As he continued to watch the scene that was set out before him, it slowly began to fade away into nothingness. Then it was gone entirely. Nothing remained but his memory of it. Turning, he saw that he was still sitting on the bench, with the stranger beside him, looking out over the Thames. He now felt as though his soul had become tarnished, positively infected by what he had just witnessed.

The Devil tapped him gently on the knee before continuing.

"What you have seen here is no dystopian imagery, shown merely to frighten and intimidate. The year was 1854 and those people were as real as you are. Though that may take some believing. Remember their plight and consider it your own." He then lapsed into silence and remained that way for some time, allowing Albert time to recover a little, and also to reflect upon what he had witnessed.

"Not very palatable, was it?" he said at last. "Though I deemed it necessary to show you those things in order to make the required point. You tread a narrow path Albert Calderwood-Brown, and the route you have chosen becomes narrower with each passing day and every step that you take. Let me ask you, is it a course you still intend to take, knowing what you have just witnessed? Albert answered with a resounding 'NO'. It was a 'no' that issued forth from the very depths of his soul, and he meant it.

"That's just what I wanted to hear!" exclaimed the Devil brightly, and tapped his knee again for good measure. Then he took something from his pocket and handed it to Albert.

"What is it?" asked the man in confusion.

"It's your bank book," replied the Devil. "It shows me that over the years you have managed to salt away quite a tidy sum. If I may be so bold, I strongly urge you, in future, to make your watchword be Restitution. Should you do this, then there is a chance of you not treading the same path of the poor unfortunates you have just witnessed here."

Albert nodded, but didn't speak. The Devil then rose from the bench.

"Do you think it will snow later? I have to say I have my doubts," he said, and slowly began to walk away before Albert could supply an answer.

After word

Albert remained sitting upon the bench for a long time after the Devil had left him. He sat gazing out over the Thames in a near zombie-like stupor. If truth be told he was in such a state of shock, he doubted very much that his legs would actually bear his weight if he stood upon them. His limbs continued to shake for some considerable time to come, and he suffered cold sweats, almost as though he had ague. It was a good hour before he felt in anyway capable of rising and making his way home again. He stumbled to his car, like a drunken man, eliciting at least two offers of help from members of the public. In both instances he kindly refused. Once back at his car he made sure to make short work of his white cane, dark spectacles and sign - all consigned to the nearest waste bin.

The following day he set out upon a new chapter of his life. This entailed going to his bank, taking out a large sum of money, and then travelling back up to London. Here, he spent the day going around, giving handouts to the needy and generally dispensing any help he could. In time to come this form of help blossomed and he joined a charitable organisation called the Action Force Volunteers, whose sole purpose was to visit the destitute and the homeless, providing hot soup and blankets. The images he had witnessed during his time with the Devil never left him. It was a constant reminder of what might have been had the strange man not intervened on his behalf.

St Paul's Cathedral

Being the 21st December – a.m.

A biting north-easterly wind had got up, as the Devil stood before St Paul's Cathedral. He hadn't been there long and he knew that he didn't have long to wait. Consulting his pocket watch, he could see it was now exactly 9.02 a.m. Looking up at the towering structure, he marvelled at the precision of the building. Dazzling in its Portland stone, it was most definitely a modern-day work of art, and no question about it. Though what he meant by modern-day was post conflagration.

"Magnificent, isn't it?" came a not totally unexpected voice from behind him.

The Devil turned to his left and looked the man up and down, and then smiled broadly; as the man could only interpret as being friendly.

"You never said a truer word, my friend," he replied. "I hope you don't mind my saying, and correct me if I'm wrong, but aren't you, Peter Hargreaves?"

The man's countenance fell, his jaw nearly touching the floor.

"Well – yes – yes, it is," he answered. "But how did you know that? I don't think we have met before, have we? I feel sure I would have remembered if we had."

The Devil laughed loudly.

"The answer is pretty explicable, Peter. It's really nothing mysterious, believe me. You see, a friend of mind recently was up this way, mainly with a view to seeing the cathedral, here. Said he met someone who proved invaluable when it came to showing him around and filling in all the little details about the place. Oddly enough he described you to a tee. Even down to your artificial leg there." At this point he gave it an inoffensive rap with his cane, the very one he had acquired yesterday. He now decided to use it more often, as he felt it added a certain something to his whole ensemble – a certain éclat if you will. "So, you see," he continued, "it's all pretty prosaic really, once you know the truth of the matter, that is."

"Yes, I suppose so," replied Peter. "Well, I was glad to be of service to your friend, whoever he is. I, hope he was happy with what I had to tell him."

The Devil nodded enthusiastically.

"He was more than happy. Why, he was over the moon, Peter, he was absolutely over the moon. Virtually beside himself he was with enthusiasm. He said you had a way of infusing historical detail with pure zeal and unadulterated delight. And it was because of this that I sort you out. I was hoping that you might be able to offer me the same service, that is if you aren't too busy at this present moment in time?"

All this outpouring of appreciation and adulation for his skills as a guide, caused Peter some embarrassment, and he said as much.

"I really only endeavour to make things a little more interesting for my clients, that's all," he explained. "I must be honest with you and tell you that I am not an official guide. The cathedral's hierarchy frowns upon people like me, I'm afraid, mainly because they charge a lot more for a tour of the old girl than I do. I only charge ten pounds, and the –"

"Ten pounds! Is that all?" interjected the Devil, appalled at this admission. "Why, that's a mere trifle! I shall pay you twenty-five pounds, and not a penny less, and that brooks no argument - and even then, I feel as though I have come out of it with a good deal. There, as I say, twenty-five pounds is what I agreed and twenty-five pounds is what I shall pay. Do we have a bargain?"

Peter took the money, though with a certain reluctance. This was way beyond what he would normally charge, and it didn't sit at all well with him. But if this gentleman wanted his expertise that badly, and was willing to pay for it, then who was he to argue? At least he would ensure that he gave full value for money, come what may.

"Should you wish to go inside the cathedral then that is an additional charge, I'm afraid," he admitted. This matter of an entrance fee into the cathedral always stuck in his craw. To begin with, he had not the wherewithal to pay for two tickets, and secondly, he knew full well it simply wasn't worth the money. In truth there was very little to see once inside, and more often than not, those that had chosen to go inside had come out feeling rather short changed. Peter felt that it was his duty to point that out and promptly did so, fully expecting his new-found customer to agree. But it shocked him when he didn't.

"I don't see that as a problem," said the Devil. "If nothing else, at least it will be dry and relatively warm inside, don't you agree?"

Peter had to concur, but then added:

"Yes, I suppose so, and it would certainly get us out of this wind, too. It's definitely picking up quite a bit."

"Ha ha. Wind? You call this a wind?" said the Devil, dismissively. "Believe me, Peter, this is nothing. You should have been here in 1703. My, now that was a wind to behold. It was the 26th November if I recall correctly. Lasted over a week it did, and caused mayhem like you can't even begin to imagine: it blew the lead off Westminster Abbey, and brought down over two thousand chimney pots throughout the city. Roof tiles were being blown about like confetti. Mind you, saying that, even that pales into insignificance when you consider the storm we had in 1091. A veritable tornado it was. My oh my, now that was a humdinger of a wind. Speeds of over 230mph - can you believe it? Fair took your breath away, it did. Did you know it levelled hundreds of houses, and blew London bridge down? Hence the old rhyme! And not to mention it took the church roof off St Mary-le-bow. It deposited it again with such force, the twenty-six-foot oak rafters were sunken into the ground with only four feet of the ends of those sticking out. It was staggering to behold." The Devil stopped mid-sentence and realised that he was getting rather a little too carried away with his recollections, which was often a bad habit of his. Peter was standing next to him with mouth partially agape. "Naturally, what I meant to say was it must have been a sight to behold, don't you think? Had you actually witnessed it, of course. Shall we go inside? It's turning a tad nippy out here, don't you think? There's talk of snow later."

The Devil paid the entrance fee, and Peter slowly, though somewhat dubiously, entered the cathedral, following on close behind.

The interior was large and chilly, as might be expected, and there were very few people about. But as it was late in the year, and so close to Christmas, then this might have been expected. Peter took charge and began showing the Devil around, explaining the history and the architecture and how Christopher Wren had been obliged to cheat somewhat when designing the dome, as no-one had any real idea as to whether it would hold up or not, due to the structural stress involved. The Devil, for his part made all the right sounds and nodded and then smiled when required to do so; having absolutely no interest in any of it, whatsoever. After all, hadn't he been here during construction? Hadn't he witnessed the on-going building works? It had been a pretty tedious fare back then if he was honest.

Finally, they found somewhere to sit, and it was readily apparent to the Devil that Peter was glad of the opportunity to do so. He looked drawn and somewhat haggard; his skin had taken on an altogether yellowish pallor. Excusing himself, he began slowly to get his breath.

"Sorry about that," he explained. "I have a bit of a liver complaint. It causes me to get a little breathless from time to time. But I'll be all right in a moment. Just need to sit down for an instant, then I'll be as right as rain. It's nothing too serious."

The Devil, who was only too aware of Peter's condition, knowing that it was terminal, and had now gone beyond conventional treatment. "You have no need to explain," he replied. "Take as long as you need. At least we are slightly warmer in here. It sounds as if it's blowing a gale out there. I tell you what, and as a brief aside, I wonder, are you at all familiar with the previous St Paul's? I mean the one that used to stand here prior to the great fire?"

Peter said that he wasn't, as no-one had ever asked him before, though he felt sure it must have been a magnificent structure and would undoubtedly have been most interesting.

"Well, let me entertain you with a few snippets of information about it," returned the Devil, warming to his task. It always gave him such a thrill when he was able to enlighten someone, be it about buildings, architecture, stories, or things that had gone on in yester years of the old capital. He regarded himself as a veritable cornucopia of information, be it useful or otherwise. "It may surprise you to learn that the cathedral that stood here, before what you see now, was in fact considerably larger than this," he said.

Peter seemed altogether surprised by this knowledge, given the size of the newer building, which in itself was nothing short of colossal.

"Well, I have to say I find that a bit hard to imagine," he said. "But if you say so."

"Oh, it's true all right. You may take my word for that," replied the Devil. "It took over two hundred years to build, can you believe, off and on, of course, and overall, it was over seventy feet taller and a whopping two hundred feet longer than the current one. It really was something to behold."

This caused Peter to shake his head in near disbelief.

"That's nothing short of incredible," he admitted. "It must have been some structure. I would have liked to have seen it."

"Oh, it was indeed," said the Devil. "Mind you, saying that, it did fall heavily into decline for various reasons throughout its existence; mainly political, which is usually the case. At the beginning of the sixteenth century, it was in such a poor state King James the first commissioned Inigo Jones to restore it. Seems ironic really when you consider it was just a few years prior to the great fire of 1666. It turned out to be a complete waste of money, man power and resources. Of course, after the fire there was nothing left of it, nothing at all, just a large pile of rubble. All rather sad really. In its heyday it really was quite something. But then everything is transient, isn't it – even us."

Peter could relate to this sentiment only too well. His condition meant that his time upon this earth was limited, and getting shorter by the day. The only reason he continued to push himself to the degree that he did, was that he had a wife and a small child to provide for. It terrified him to think that they would be alone and without support once he was gone. Looking up, he saw that his charge was now staring at him in a rather odd way; though it had to be said a very compassionate one. It was a scrutinous gaze, almost as if the man could see all his problems and his pain, and yet was altogether in complete sympathy with him concerning them. Empathy seemed to radiate from him, like a warm satisfying light. It bathed and filled his inner being with a comfort that felt as though it was touching his very soul. Then, all of a sudden, it was gone again, leaving Peter to believe it was simply his over-active imagination playing tricks on him, brought on by his present level of exhaustion.

The Devil smiled again and then suggested, as he was feeling rather tired from all his exploits, that they went for a quick bite to eat. At first Peter declined, not having the wherewithal to pay for such delights; but the Devil insisted, claiming that as they both were feeling below par then it was the very least he could do in light of the excellent service he had received for the tour. Eventually Peter acquiesced, though not feeling as though he had properly earned it in any way. He was instinctively aware that the Devil was showing him a kindness he felt that he didn't rightly deserve, though he had no wish to offend the man.

Leaving the cathedral, they both pulled their respective coats up around their necks, so as to ward off the severe wind that had now got up. The Devil led the way, and very soon they found themselves warmly ensconced in a small restaurant just off the main thoroughfare. Peter looked slightly puzzled by it.

"You know," he remarked, "I am most familiar with this area, but I cannot for the life of me ever recall seeing this place before."

"I think it's fairly new," answered the Devil, knowing full well that up to a few moments ago it hadn't even existed. "I'm told the food is pretty good. And I'm sure we could both do with something warming after all that exercise. It's bitterly cold out there. Or to use more common parlance, I believe it is known as 'taters' here." This caused him to chuckle loudly.

Peter laughed also and had to agree.

"It's certainly a cold one today. I'm sure, if truth be told most people would prefer to be at home in the warm. It is only necessity that brings us out on a day like this."

The Devil nodded and heartily concurred. After scanning the menu, they ordered a light lunch. It was at that point the Devil broached the subject of Peter's ailment, obviously feeling little or no embarrassment about doing so. Generally, it was a subject that Peter preferred to avoid, especially with strangers. He expected no pity for his condition and wanted none either. It paid to play your cards close to your chest in life, he found, and that is what he generally did.

"So," asked the Devil a trifle forthrightly, "what exactly is ailing you? That is if you don't mind my asking. It is very obvious to anyone with an eye that all is not well."

Immediately, Peter began to dismiss the question, feeling it was too much of an intrusion.

"It's really nothing worth talking about," he replied. "Just one of those things that I would prefer to keep to myself, if you don't mind."

Full expecting his host to agree and apologise for the imposition, he was somewhat surprised when the Devil replied:

"Oh, but I do mind, Peter. You see I mind very much. I would like to know, which is why I asked, and I would like you to tell me," he said in a most disarming way, with his hands placed just below his chin and his head tilted slightly to one side, smiling for all the world as though he meant no invasion of privacy what so ever.

It would be untrue to say that Peter wasn't both shocked and surprised by this uninvited intrusion and, not to put too fine a point on it, was also rather dismayed by it as well. He hesitated initially at the request, and had intended to be rather curt in his response, but then, for reasons unbeknown to himself, he found that he was pouring out his whole life to this man. The Devil sat quietly, taking in everything that was imparted to him. Peter told him of his spell in the armed forces, meeting the girl of his dreams, the daughter they now had – and then the shock and horror of being diagnosed with a particular form of cancer that was incurable. The very telling of it caused him to feel drained and weary. When he had finished his story, he sat waiting for a response from this altogether strange man sitting opposite, this man who had somehow caused him to reveal everything there was to know about himself.

Taking out a leather wallet, the Devil proceeded to remove a small card from it. Slipping it across the table, he enlightened Peter, by saying:

"This is a personal friend of mine. He owes me a favour – or two. I would like you to give him a call straight away, today in fact. The sooner the better. I feel sure he will be able to help you."

Taking the card, Peter held it up and read it. "Professor J.H.Tillman – Oncologist." He looked surprised. "He's based in Harley Street."

The Devil nodded and sipped his coffee.

"Yes, he's quite the leader in his field actually. One of the best, in fact. A good chap to know in a pinch. Tailor-made for people such as yourself. As I say, you really shouldn't delay. I will give him the heads up that you intend to call – the sooner the better. Go along and have a chat with him. You have nothing to lose and possibly an awful lot to gain."

Peter turned the card over several times in his hands, unsure of what to make of it all.

"If your friend resides in Harley Street then he must be pretty expensive," he said at last.

"Expensive? Yes, he is. Exorbitant, in fact!" replied the Devil. "Have the very shirt off your back, if you let him. That was a joke by the way. Excuse my waggish tone. Yes, he's expensive, but that because he's the best."

Slipping the card back across the table Peter said.

"That is very kind of you, but I do not think I could run to the man's costs – "

The Devil held up a hand and silenced Peter.

"As I said, he's an old friend of mine and owes me one or two things. You do not need to worry over the cost of your visit. Call it an early Christmas present, if you will." Raising his coffee cup, he added, "A toast – to you Peter – good health and a very long life."

Not knowing quite how to react to this, or what he should say, Peter raised his cup and offered the greetings of the season, and then added.

"I thank you for your kindness, Nick, however I can't help feeling it will be a pointless visit. All the tests I have had so far point to the fact that –"

Once again, the Devil stopped him mid-sentence.

"Tests – tests – tests! Pah - stuff and nonsense!" he began. "If I were to tell you of the percentage of so called 'Tests' that are wholly inaccurate, you would find it hard to believe. Trust me on this. If you want to learn what's really going on, then consult someone who knows precisely what they are talking about. Now, let's hear no more of it, here's our lunch, if I am not mistaken. And most hearty it looks, too. Why, I believe, this should put a spring in our step, before we are obliged to go out into the cold, once more and battle the elements."

It was difficult not to concur. The food looked excellent and tasted even better. Once he had finished clearing his plate, Peter felt altogether healthier, both mentally and physically. Hard to think that this could be brought about by a simple plate of food, but it did. But then, he wasn't aware of the Devil's added ingredient that made it so.

Eventually it was time for the parting of the ways. They called for their coats and began to muffle themselves against the severe weather that lay just a short distance outside. Opening the door to the restaurant, they were both pleasantly surprised to see that the wind had dropped, and what was more, it was now snowing, quite heavily in fact. It caused the Devil to smile.

"Well, I never!" he exclaimed heartily, "It would seem that Christmas has finally arrived. And not before time, too."

They both turned up the collars on their coats and Peter took the Devil's hand and shook it with a warmth and a gratitude that could not be mistaken.

"I will do as you ask regarding your friend," he said. "You have my word that I shall ring him after Christmas –"

For the third time that morning the Devil interposed, and a raised finger, cutting Peter off short.

"No, Peter, you will ring him before you do anything else. I shall do the same in order to pave the way for you. Never prevaricate when things need attending to. It never ever pays, believe me."

And with that he gave him a jovial slap on the shoulder, turned, and began making his way along the street. Peter watched him go, not knowing quite what to make of the man. But did it matter? Nick had shown him a rare kindness, and he felt a whole lot better for it, even if it was only of a psychological nature.

After word

True to his word, Peter waited until the Devil was out of sight and then telephoned the number on the card. It shocked him to learn, when the receptionist announced that Professor Tillman had been awaiting his call. Once through, he learnt that Professor Tillman had already been fully informed of his situation and stressed that he would like to see him immediately. Being so late in the year, and so close to Christmas, this announcement stunned Peter to the core. He immediately rang his wife and explained, to the best of his ability, what had happened. She, too, found it hard to assimilate and take on board, but was excited nevertheless, always believing that there was hope.

During that afternoon, Peter kept his appointment, as promised, and was duly subjected to a number of tests, the results of which the Professor promised to have back by the following day at the very latest. True to his word, on the afternoon of the 22nd he rang Peter at home and announced that every test that had been carried out had come back negative. He was therefore given a clean bill of health. This news had to be incorrect and Peter said as much. He'd had numerous tests before, and on many occasions, and they had all diagnosed the same. Professor Tillman, however, was insistent that there was nothing wrong with him and suggested he return to his own GP in the New Year for clarification. He said that he was more than willing to send over the results, should they request them.

Peter was left altogether at a loss as to what was going on. How was any of this possible? There was no way that it could be. Once he informed his wife as to the Professor's findings, she too, found it nearly all too much to comprehend and was forced to sit down to take it all in.

Following the best Christmas, they had had in a very long time, Peter did indeed contact his GP and explained in great detail what had happened. His GP was left utterly bemused by the news and then arranged for further tests to be carried out at Peter's local hospital. Sure enough, as soon as the results were in, it merely clarified what Professor Tillman had already deduced: Peter was as healthy as a butcher's dog.

No Gooders

Being the 21st December – p.m.

The Devil sauntered at an altogether unhurried pace along Fleet Street, and then on into the Strand. Consulting his pocket watch, he knew that he was in plenty of time for his next rendezvous. And so, as was his won't at this time year, especially when he got the opportunity to do so, he spent his time looking at all the shops he passed - though never actually going in, of course. An innocuous pastime, without question, but one that gave him a great deal of pleasure nevertheless. The feeling he got at this time of year, which was a warm, upbeat vibrancy, passed over him like a wave, as it so often did at Christmas. He stopped, mid-stride, overcome with it all. Taking out a crisply ironed handkerchief from his coat-pocket, he wiped his eye with it.

In all walks of life, incidents will often occur, that will put a damper on things. And now was no exception. Having secreted his handkerchief in his coat pocket, the Devil moved on again, only to nearly bowled over by a young boy. He was around ten years of age and had run smack bang into him, falling to the floor in the process. The

Devil bent forward and took hold of the lad by the scruff of the neck and hoisted him aloft.

"In a bit of a hurry, aren't we?" he said.

The boy had, clutched in his hand, two items of apparel; they were designer labels by the look of them, and what's more they were still on their hangers – with price tags intact. There was little or no doubt that he had stolen them from the store and was making good his escape, when he had bumped into possibly the worst person he could have.

"Well, well," continued the Devil upon seeing the items. "And what might we have here then, young man? Purloined articles? A tea-leaf, I believe, is the common parlance, is it not?"

The boy, a rough looking individual, with no soft edges about him at all, gave the Devil a withering look and barked out loudly.

"Let me go! It ain't none of your business what I'm doing, you nosey bleedin' parker! Put me down, or I'll have the law on you!"

"Mm, I somehow doubt it." re-joined the Devil, and looked the lad up and down with a severe and scrutinous eye. Definitely a candidate for the fiery pit, this one, that is unless he chose to change his ways, and what's more sooner than later, he thought. "Been up to no good, I see."

At this juncture a large and very lumbering security guard came running out of the store. He was breathing heavily, as though he had been chasing the lad the length and breath of the building. The Devil noticed that the man was rather over weight and most certainly out of condition and was not well suited to chasing young imps about the locality. But then each and everyone was allotted their role in life – so, who was he to judge, even though he invariably did?

"Thanks," said the guard, taking a deep breath, before grabbing the lad from the Devil. "I've been after him for days. Comes in here, lifts a number of items, on a near daily basis, and then he's off again, like a bloody hare. I've almost lost my job over this little sod."

The lad began to squirm in the guard's vice-like grip, though in all truth, he had no chance of breaking free.

"Let me go!" he bawled; his screams began to cause quite a scene. Those shoppers in close proximity stopped their perambulations and looked over to see what was going on. "I've got friends! And they won't like it if they know what you've done!" he continued to yell at the top of his voice. "Let me go!"

"As to you having friends, though I believe the term confederates would be a better choice of words, I have little or no doubt whatsoever," said the Devil. "Would these friends, possibly, be 'Jimmy the Slip' and 'Markie and the Toad', at all?"

The lad's face broke into an immediate expression of exposed vulnerability. It spoke volumes of how he was feeling right then, looking bare and vulnerable as if his whole world had just been laid exposed for everyone to see. It was not a pleasant sight to behold.

"How do you know them?" he asked, incredulously.

Leaning much closer, the Devil answered quietly in the lad's ear.

"Have no fear young Robert, for I am only too familiar with your friends and, not only that but much more besides. Their current activities are well known to me, believe me. I have been watching them for some considerable time now. Let me assure you that they will all get a very personal visit from me in good time – every last one of them, and that's a promise."

Having the lad firmly by his collar, so there was no possibility of escape, the security guard thanked the Devil for being so alert and said that he wished how it would make his job so much easier if other members of the public would be a little more vigilant.

"If you would come with me, sir," he said. "Only we need to take a brief statement from you, so as to show precisely what happened here. It shouldn't take too long."

Once again, the Devil leaned forward, covert fashion, and looked deep into the guard's eyes.

"I don't think so," he said, and the announcement brooked no argument in the matter.

The guard, was a trifle surprised by the rebuffal, and quickly followed up his request with a statement that he hoped sounded a great deal more officious.

"Well, we'll need your address, at the very least," he said. "The Police will need to contact you about it."

Shaking his head, the Devil replied.

"I somehow rather doubt that any address I gave would prove to be of any great help to them. No post code, you see."

And saying that, he moved off up the street, leaving both guard and boy in a thorough state of utter befuddlement.

Tipping his hat to Christmas shoppers and smiling at everyone he passed, the Devil found that he was completely in his element. Such good humour and general bon homie, he noted. It was sufficient to die for.

Having made his way up the Strand and into the Charing Cross Road, and then on into Leicester Square, he paused and took in everything that the square had to offer. A huge Christmas tree stood central stage, all brightly lit up, flashing its message of seasonal cheer and what's more making a wonderful central feature. A present from Norway, who had been providing a tree every year since nineteen forty-seven. Beneath this were grouped the Salvation Army, all vocally ebullient and singing carols, ruddy faces all aglow, and all the while adding their own personal feelings of good will to one and all. It was a most joyous occasion, and everyone present felt the benevolence that laced the very air with its magic.

Meandering his way through the Christmas market, viewing all the diverse options of food and drink from all the various countries of Europe; hats, coats, gloves and warm jumpers, all bedecked in seasonal colours and design. There was so much going on, so much to take in, for a brief moment he nearly forgot why he was there. Then, as he viewed the crowd, it became all too obvious why this place was on his list. Anyone else, looking at the milling throng of people, all intent on having a good time, would not have noticed anything amiss, and why would they? But he most certainly did. His eyes narrowed and shot back and forth, taking in every last detail of what was transgressing before him. Within the crowd were five individuals who were intent on bringing misery to as many people as they could at Christmas time. They were an organised gang of pick-pockets, not unlike Nobby Bracknell in many ways, but only on a much grander, and more sophisticated scale. And they were good, yes, they were very good; well organised, adroit and fast. As he watched them going about their business of misappropriation, which had to be said was impressive in its execution, he realized that they were like a well-oiled machine; first the dip, followed by an immediate swap, followed by a second and then a third. So sharp, so efficient, it was difficult not to have a certain admiration for all their efforts. Though, of course, he didn't. The gang consisted of two men and three young woman, each and every one of them fully conversant with what was expected of them. The last of the women was wearing a voluminous over coat, no doubt to conceal the wallets, purses and phones her two male colleagues were stealing from members of the public. Each item had to be small and of value. All very easy to offload.

Watching them going about their iniquitous exploits made the Devil's ire begin to rise. Not that anyone would have been aware of this by watching him. To all intents and purpose, he was merely just another shopper enjoying the Christmas ambience.

As he continued to view their wrong doings, his escalating fury began to course through his veins like a sulphurous ichor; burning intensely, it was seeking redress. It had to be said that this was the one aspect of his job that he truly loathed, metering out retribution to those who neither wanted it, but deserved it nevertheless. And like it or not, that was what he was about to do. So, slowly making his way through the crowd towards one of the young men, he waited until he had picked an elderly man's pocket, then in one swift movement he had stuck out his foot and upended the thief. Down went the man in a heap, sprawling amongst the slush and mud that had been churned up by so many Christmas shoppers. The young man slowly began to get to his feet, assuming it was just an accident caused by the sheer size of the crowd, but as he did so the Devil moved forward, took him by the sleeve of his coat and whispered in his ear, "You've been rumbled, my friend." The effect was instantaneous. At once the man broke free and ran. The Devil did nothing whatsoever to stop him. Looking up he saw the other members of the gang, fully aware that something was amiss, they now began to revert to form. Everyone one of them slowly began to peel off in different directions, not wishing to bring any attention to themselves. This too, didn't worry the Devil in the slightest. After all, there was always more than one way to skin a cat, and time never felt constrained to pose a problem for him.

The first man to have been accosted by the Devil took off as though the very hounds of hell were hot on his tail. And had he been aware of the truth of the matter, he would most definitely not have felt so confident in thinking he was making good his escape. Shooting down a side street, where there were few Christmas shoppers and revellers, he turned and looked back to see if he was being followed. Seeing that all appeared clear, he slowed his pace a little and breathed a sigh of relief. That was close. He wondered if perhaps it was simply a member of the public who had seen him lift the old man's wallet, or an undercover policeman. Either way, it made little difference. The haul had been a good one, today. And the night was still young. As prearranged, should this situation ever occur, they would all meet up later at one of many cafés, or bar's they frequented and make further plans, seemingly like a group of innocuous friends merely enjoying Christmas together. At least he had the old man's wallet – or so he thought. Patting his pocket to confirm this, he was a little surprised to learn that it appeared to have gone. Going through his pocket, he cursed his luck. It had indeed disappeared. Could he have dropped it in his desire to get away? That was the only thing that made sense.

Back in Leicester Square, the Devil was in the process of replacing the wallet with even more dexterity than which it had originally been taken. The elderly man, totally unaware of what had transpired, felt absolutely nothing whatsoever. Having put right the misdemeanour, the Devil then moved on.

Having finally come to terms with his annoyance, and anger at himself, for apparently having dropped the wallet, whilst making good his escape, the young man continued on towards his rendezvous with his friends. As he made his way along the street, it suddenly became obvious to him that he didn't recognize where he was. The buildings appeared to have changed totally. This was very odd, he thought and assumed that he had taken a wrong turning and had gone the wrong way. Looking back, he fully expected to see Leicester Square, but that too was now completely different, and seemingly altered in the extreme. But how could that be? He must have inadvertently taken a turning he was not used to in his eagerness to get away. That had to be the answer, and it was really the only logical explanation for how he now found himself somewhere totally unknown to him. The street curved round towards the left. He chose to follow it. There was no-one around, not a solitary soul, which also struck him as being rather peculiar. Then, without any warning, he saw one of the girls from his group, Karri, emerged from a building and beckoned him quickly towards her. What would she be doing here? That wasn't part of their plan. As he watched, she then quickly slipped back inside. The young man couldn't make out what she was doing there, but didn't think to question it any further. No doubt there would be a perfectly rational explanation for it. All would soon be made clear.

Crossing the street, he checked all around to ensure that he wasn't being followed, then he too slipped inside the building. There were no lights on anywhere; and at first, he thought that he had gained access to an office complex of some sort, though as to what it was doing still open at this time of night he couldn't even begin to imagine. He called out 'Karri'; silently at first, just to ensure he wasn't alerting anyone else to his presence, then, when he received no reply, called her name even more loudly. Again, there was no response. As he listened intently for any sign of where she may have gone a door just slightly off to one side banged quietly shut. That must be where she had gone. He chose to follow just to be sure.

Once through the door, he found himself in a large well-lit room, but was alarmed, and then horrified to see the other four members of his group all seated in a semi-circle in the middle of a very large room. They were all facing a bearded man who was seated upon what looked like an ornate throne of sorts. None of his friends seemed able to speak, or even move for that matter, and all appeared to be in an acute state of catatonia. The bearded man looked up, then smiled widely and beckoned him forward. It was then and only then he realised it was the same man from earlier, the self-same man who had caught him stealing the old man's wallet. What was going on here?

"Alan!" the man called out brightly, "Please come and join your friends, here. We were just getting to know one another whilst waiting for you. So glad you could make it. And now that you have made it the set is complete and we can begin our little chat."

The whole scenario set out before him was altogether surreal, as if it had been magicked up by some wizard. What he couldn't quite make out was how it was that this guy knew his name? Who was he? And what were all the others doing here? And why did they all appear to be asleep? This felt very much as if he were being led into a trap; though he also felt induced to join the others and sit in the chair that had been left vacant for him, almost as if he were going through the motions of a script for a play he was in, only this was very real. Sitting quietly, he looked at his friends with ever growing concern. They all sat staring straight ahead, eyes agog, as if they had witnessed something truly terrifying and were now paralysed with fear and unable to communicate or move.

The scene made him shiver in dread, both at what he was seeing, but more an inherent feeling he now had of what was to come.

"How do you know me?" he asked the Devil, who had continued smiling throughout the proceedings, without an apparent concern in the world.

"A mere bagatelle," he responded, smoothly. "It's hardly worth the explanation, believe me. What is important is that we are all here together; you, me and the rest of your associates here. In your absence I have been getting to know them, really quite intimately, while we waited for you, that is." He then proceeded to point them all out one at a time. "There's Kerri, Roger, and the Dolly twins. And of course, not forgetting yourself, Alan. How could I ever forget you? As you have already gathered, I have spoken at length with every one here before your arrival. We were going through all of their past misdemeanours, crimes, transgressions and general wrong-doings – of which, it has to be said, it is quite a rather substantial catalogue. Fairly took my breath away, to be frank with you. Which takes a lot of doing, believe me! And now it is time to go through your list of indiscretions, Alan. Let me assure you that it makes for very interesting reading and viewing. Though, it has to said, I am altogether disappointed that someone of your upbringing and general background has descended to this. But I digress, and that never pays now, does it? If you would please be so good as to look closely at the small spot you see before you there on the floor. Yes, that's right, the small glowing red spot that appears to be getting larger as you view it."

As Alan stared at the small spot, which looked to him as if it were part of the pattern on the tiles, he saw that it began to move and fluctuate. It throbbed, pulsated and began to spread wider, and as it spread a light appeared to issue forth from its centre, a dull red choking radiance that seemed to come with its own threatening brume. Alan continued to watch in rising horror as it appeared to spread ever wider, until it had reached the very tips of his toes which were firmly placed upon the stone floor before him. Looking down, he saw he was now gazing into what appeared to be a vast fiery pit, that looked as if it descended on forever. Issuing forth from the pit there came a series of soul-searing melancholy screams, screams that rose to the top of the pit and then faded away again, only to be repeated time and again, as though it were the cries of the damned. Flames roared and belched, and an overwhelming stench, so fetid it made him want to wretch, filled his nasal cavities throughout. It was all he could do to remain on the chair, which he now gripped, vice-like, as it seemed the only thing he could do that gave him a lifeline to any form of sanity.

The Devil moved a little closer to his side and gave his chair a gentle nudge forward, causing Alan to shriek aloud.

"Woops! That was close, wasn't it, Alan? Perhaps a little too close for comfort, hmm?" he said. "Not at all appealing, is it? I mean, it doesn't look at all alluring, does it, what with all those screams issuing forth from those poor unfortunate lost souls and those who have been cursed?"

Alan couldn't respond, he was now so gripped with a terror so profound he was convinced that he was about to pass out. "Naturally." continued the Devil, "your friends here have already seen this, that was just before you happened to show up – don't you just loath repeats? I know I do. Anyhow, they reacted to it very much like you are doing now, which I have to say I found completely understandable, given the circumstances. Believe me when I say, the abyss takes quite a bit of getting used to; and it also has to be said that not many of those who witness this scene often do that."

Taking a quivering Alan by the scruff of the neck, the Devil hoisted him aloft and held him precariously above the pit, so that his feet were literally hanging just above the fiery rim.

"Are you at all familiar with Dante Alighieri, Alan?" continued the Devil. "He wrote a very famous book, entitled 'The Divine comedy'. It's about one man's descent into hell. A most interesting read, if I was honest with you. And in all fairness to Mr Alighieri, he managed to get a lot of it right first time, too; which surprised me a great deal, especially when one considers that he had never actually been there before. Anyhow, I'm allowing myself to stray again. A particular weakness of mine, I may add. As I was about to say, all I would need to do is to loosen my grip a little and down you would go – down – down – down – a continual descent into who knows what? Not a pleasant thought at all. It's funny, you know, but rarely in my experience do people ever willingly change for the better. It always takes something like this to veritably shock the system into some form of wakefulness. After that, they can usually get to grips and 'smell the coffee' as it were – and it's usually pretty well roasted too by that time, if down there's anything to go by, that is. Now, what I would like you to do, if you would be so good, is to focus your eyes most carefully upon that poor wretch just over there in the far corner; can you see, that one to the left of that headless individual; can you see him against the far wall? There, where that rock juts out all covered in human internal organs? Ghastly, isn't it? Well, that poor wretch is you, Alan - yes that's right, and you're endeavouring as best as you can, against near overwhelming odds I may add, to climb up that ladder secured to the wall in order to get out of the pit. Even though the odds are most definitely stacked against it. They say the house always wins, don't they? Now, watch closely what happens. You should find this quite interesting. I know I always do. It's a real blast."

Alan had no choice, his eyes were drawn inexorably to this nightmarish image being played out before him; he saw a vision of himself, desperately trying to climb out of the hellish pit, grappling, screaming, pulling, wrenching, anything to escape. As he watched, he could clearly see another vision that opened up before him, of an elderly woman. He seemed to be approaching her from behind, trying to remove her purse from her hand-bag, which was hooked across her shoulder. The woman sensed what was happening and turned, and then desperately began trying to pull the bag from his grip. Knowing that the game was up, he forcibly knocked her to the ground, grabbed the bag and took off. The vision instantly evaporated, leaving Alan still holding onto the ladder, which had now come away from the wall, and still desperately trying to climb out. Every time he ascended one rung, he found himself two rungs further down. And regardless of what he did, his descent was assured: one up, followed by two down – sometimes it was three, but down he went, notwithstanding, each bad action he performed resulted in him being dragged further and further into the pit.   He watched and saw himself screaming loudly, frantic to get out, but regardless of what he did a downward descent was always inevitable, his fate inexorable.

"That's the way it works," said the Devil, sounding very matter of fact about it all. "Some call it, karma, others say it is merely providence; destiny if you like, or even just being the way of things. Either way, you always end up reaping what you sow. It's just how things are done in the grand scheme of things; it's a universal law. Nothing, no matter how small, is ever overlooked, believe me. I now have to point out to you something that could turn out to be your saving grace here, so I would suggest that you take heed and pay very close attention to what I have to say." Alan couldn't have done anything else at that precise moment in time; rigid with fear, he felt like a rag-doll in the Devil's grip. The Devil promptly continued with his narrative: "There comes a time in many people's lives when they are obliged to stop and take stock of themselves, to look inwardly, if you like, and to fully assess their true worth in the world. Very often it is not a pleasant experience, and a lot of the time I am called upon to show them exactly what they do not wish to see. Just as I have done with you, now, to be more precise. So many times, people will have come too far along life's dusty pathway to be able to administer any change whatsoever in their lives. The sheer scale of what is required of them is just too overwhelming. They then reach a point of no return. And the inevitable consequences of that is what you now see before you. Let me ask you, Alan, do you feel as if you have reached that point of no return in your life? I must emphasise, it really does pay to be honest here as an awful lot depends upon it."

Alan felt a sudden constricting sensation beginning to work its way relentlessly up his body; it started from the very bottom of his toes, and ended at the very top of his head. Unable to speak, he could only shake his head, which he proceeded to do most vigorously. Professing not to understand what he was saying, the Devil shook him again, quite violently.

"What was that?" he asked, pulling Alan a little closer to him.

Alan began to whimper. It was quite a pathetic scene to behold. "NO!" he finally managed to squeak, almost imperceptibly and with great effort on his part.

"Couldn't quite make that out," said the Devil, again professing not to understand, and then lifted him even higher in order to grasp more clearly what he said.

With his throat getting drier and hoarser by the second, being the result of both the fear he was experiencing and the near overwhelming, suffocating sulphurous heat that arose from the pit, Alan croaked "NO!" as loudly as he could. Which, had to be said, was not that loud.

Once again, the Devil claimed not to comprehend a word.

"Alan, I would like you to take a moment and cast your mind back to your youth. Tell me, do you remember that time long long ago when you were scared of the dark? Absolutely terrified you were. Yes, you do? That's good. Your parents would often tell you at that point that there was nothing really to fear and that the dark was nothing at all to worry about, and that ghosts, ghouls and witches – and why, even the Devil himself, didn't really exist. Do you remember that? Yes, of course, you do. Excellent. Well, I have to inform you, Alan - they were wrong on all accounts."

Without another word he cast the young man casually into the pit, allowing him to fall down and out of sight.

Curiously, for a man who couldn't find his voice only seconds earlier, he certainly appeared to find it now. The screams that filled the air as he fell into the vertiginous fiery hell hole seemed to go on forever. The Devil, knowing his work here was now done, and also not giving a hoot to boot, casually turned and left.

After word

Alan fell for what seemed like an eternity – spiralling forever down he went, through the searing heat, not knowing if he would ever reach the bottom. Not daring to open his eyes, for fear of what might assail his senses. As he fell, blood curdling screams became ever more prominent. Occasionally, he would bump into something, or someone, and claw like talons would appear to rape and draw on his clothes and flesh, and then he would continue to fall again; this went on for what seemed like forever.

Without warning, he suddenly hit the ground with a resounding THUD! The first thing he became aware of was the intense cold; this was quickly followed by a wet sensation as it began to seep into his clothes. This was not what he might have been expected from the deepest pit of Hell. Slowly opening his eyes, he could see very little to begin with, just darkness, and he found himself sitting in a bank of snow. Getting up, he looked around and realized that he appeared to be in a very large field, or at least something very similar. It was snowing heavily, and in the distance, he could see lights and hear traffic from far off roads. And although he didn't know it, he was now firmly established right in the middle of Richmond Park – and what's more he was all alone.

As for his colleagues, well, they all found themselves dotted about hither and thither, the seeming length and breadth of the good old capital, and even beyond; Kerri woke up to find herself on the beach at Southend. And to make matters worse the tide was coming in and she was soaked through to the skin; Roger found himself lying facedown upon a large stone crypt, which was right in the middle of Highgate Cemetery. As for the Dolly twins, having hardly ever been separated since birth, they now found themselves one at either end of the Metropolitan line – which, had to be said, was quite a distance apart.

Concerning all the items the group had spent that very evening purloining from innocent members of the public, they were all miraculously returned to their rightful owners, none of whom were any the wiser as to their initial loss.

The Devil, for his part, had a slow saunter back to Leicester Square. The air miraculously seemed a lot clearer there now he thought to himself, almost as though a murky pall had been lifted from the place. After purchasing a particularly large and satisfying mince pie, and not to mention a hot beverage, he returned to where the Salvation Army were still engaged singing carols by the large Christmas tree, and joined them in singing as loudly and as boisterously as he could. What a wonderful and satisfying evening it had been, he thought.

The Good Samaritan

Being still the 21st December – Late Evening

Taking out his watch, the Devil quickly consulted it, and snapping it shut again, returned it to his pocket. Time to be on the move. His next meeting was around Waterloo, and he had decided to walk there, as opposed to getting the underground. Far too festive to be underground, was his opinion, so off he set.

The journey was only just over a mile, so it wouldn't take him longer than twenty minutes, or so, at most. Returning to the Charing Cross Road, he headed due south. This took him passed St Martins-in-the-Field and then along the Strand. Once there he hopped across Waterloo Bridge and was at his destination in no time at all. Taking out his watch, he checked the time again. Eighteen minutes from start to finish. "Pretty good," he said so himself.

This part of London was a far less of a hive of activity than Leicester Square, and especially so at this time of the evening. It was a place where, when darkness fell, a certain type of individual would take to the streets. Most men might have thought twice before setting out for any type of assignation here, but then of course the Devil wasn't most men. Skipping lightly across the road, without a care, he turned into Mepham Street. This was a small side street just off the main thoroughfare and it played host to mainly offices and also a small warehouse. It was this warehouse to which the Devil now headed.

As he crossed the street, his clothing straight away changed; gone was the astrakhan coat, patent leather shoes, cane and leather gloves, to be replaced with jeans, large boots, an overcoat and a large woolly hat. He thought this more in keeping with the role he was about to play.

Parked directly outside the small warehouse was a large black van. The rear doors were wide open and a man, with one arm, appeared to be directing two other people from the warehouse. They were carrying various items and depositing them into the van. Anyone of a suspicious nature might rightly have thought that they were robbing the place. The Devil, however, knew different. Approaching the one-armed man, he asked politely:

"Excuse me, are you by chance Roger Melrose?"

The man stopped his activities and looked up.

"Er, yes, that's me. Can I help you?" he asked, curiously looking the odd stranger up and down.

The Devil smiled warmly and extended a hand.

"Yes, I'm Nick. Flora from the office contacted me earlier and said you were in need of another pair of hands for the evening, so here I am."

Roger's countenance lit up and he shook the Devil's hand warmly.

"That's excellent news, Nick! If truth be told, we are a couple of people down tonight; they're both off with the flu, can you believe? Any help we can get is greatly appreciated I can tell you. I have a feeling it's going to be a long night ahead, and the weather appears to be getting worse. Come and meet the rest of the gang. This is Dan, he does most of the driving, as – well you can probably make out for yourself I'm not really up to it. And that's Ruth, my second in command. She keeps me in order and firmly on track."

"Well, someone has to," remarked Ruth, with a grin. "And anyway, as I've always said, he needs a good right arm."

They all laughed at this and shook hands cordially. The Devil then asked what was required of him as he was more than willing to chip in.

"Follow me," said Dan, "and then grab as much as you can and throw it in the back of the van."

"We don't throw things," reproved Ruth, laughing. "We place things, delicately, so it makes our life easier when we get to where we are going."

Dan winked at the Devil and said:

"You'll see soon enough."

The three of them entered the warehouse, while Roger remained with the van. Inside there was an assortment of trestle tables, each containing blankets, large thermoses and a huge assortment of clothes (all used). The warehouse was old, dilapidated and in need of much restoration, but in its present state it obviously sufficed. After a further fifteen minutes of loading up the van, Roger announced that due to the lack of space, that was all they would be able to carry. A further trip was mooted, but as the time was getting on, and not forgetting that the snow was already coming down handsomely, it was agreed that one would have to do. So off they set, Roger and Dan in the front and Ruth and the Devil in the rear.

"It isn't far," announced Roger. "Though it has to be said, parking is usually of a premium, so let's hope that lady luck is on our side."

"Or even the luck of the Devil," said the Devil, smiling, knowing full well that all would be fine.

"Have you ever done any of this sort of charitable work before?" Ruth asked him.

"No, not as such," he replied, and then added. "Bits and pieces mainly; here and there, you know how it is. Just trying to do my bit; helping out the needy and whatnot."

"We've been going for just over eight years now," said Roger. "ACTION AID," is what we call ourselves. We are a registered charity, but it has to be said our donations are pretty non-existent, really – it's down to who we know mainly that keeps us going. We trudge along, though it isn't easy."

Ruth added:

"Yes, we have tried getting a grant, to help with the running costs, but we have never managed to be successful. Though we keep pegging away. It's just a question of time before our luck turns. And I firmly believe that. God will provide a way, of that, I'm sure."

"The eternal optimist." laughed Roger. "There's no such thing as a free meal in this life, unless it's provided by us, of course – and there's no such thing as God or the Devil, either."

Which caused the Devil to mutter beneath his breath. "Wrong on both accounts."

"Unfortunately, there are too many needy people," voiced Dan, sadly. "And it's getting worse each year. Heartbreaking it is; makes you want to weep sometimes, seeing some of the worst cases. We do our best, though at times it just seems like a drop in the ocean. And there's so much to do."

Roger and Ruth agreed, but even so, all unanimously decided that it was a worthy cause and they would carry on doing it, come what may, for as long as providence provided.

"We are almost there, Nick," said Roger. "And I think that I had better mention that although we are here to help, a few of the people we meet aren't always what you might call too friendly. Circumstances having conspired to make them what they are, so we have to be careful."

Dan roared with laughter.

"That's, saying something! The truth is, it's not unusual for the odd one to get violent and take the occasional poke at you. You have to be on your metal, if you know what I mean. Always be on your guard – and never turn your back on one of them – ever!"

"Syringes are the worst hazard," said Ruth. "We have to be very careful about those, especially where heavy drugs are concerned. They really are our worst concern and you can never be too careful."

"Concern? Nightmare, she means!" added Dan.

The Devil nodded in complete and utter agreement.

"Yes, I fully understand what you are saying. But don't concern yourself, I will endeavour to be most vigilant at all times."

Roger announced that they were here, and Dan pulled over and parked the van. Then Roger explained to the Devil:

"There are numerous walk-ways that run beneath the roads hereabouts," he said. "It's a bit like a maze to be honest; just the very act of crossing from one side to the next can be an arduous undertaking. During the day, many homeless people inhabit these places and spend the daylight hours accosting people on their way to work, for money. As you can imagine, it can get a bit wearing when you get asked by as many as fifteen people one after the other for cash. And being in such a desperate state of affairs, I'm afraid they don't always think about the nicer points of being polite when they do. Some of them can get very aggressive; they try and intimidate people for hand-outs. But people soon wise up to the situation and then usually find a different route to get to work, somewhere that takes them away from the underpasses. When it gets too bad the police will then make the odd appearance and the homeless get moved on. But of course, it's only temporary. Later on, after the police have gone, they return. It's a bit of a vicious circle, I'm afraid, and one without any sign of an end."

Opening the rear of the van, they then all armed themselves with everything that they had bundled into it, a short time earlier. Dan and the Devil carried the bulky items, such as the blankets, and Roger and Ruth carried the large thermos flasks containing hot soup.

"We shall need to make about three trips," announced Roger, taking the lead. "At least if we are able to. The weather seems to be getting worse. We don't want to run the risk of getting snowed in."

The snow now began to come down much heavier as they made their way to the first underpass. The pavement was slippery and they were obliged to tread carefully as they went. Upon reaching the entrance, it became evident that a strong wind was blowing through it. A number of the lights that normally lit this area weren't working, having been smashed by vandals, and the place felt dark, dismal and gloomy; graffiti covered the walls and the place smelled heavily of urine. It was all too easy to see why most people who were obliged to work in the area avoided this place like the plague and found themselves alternative ways to get to work. A number of mattresses were placed in a line along the floor of the underpass, all of them were filthy and not fit for purpose. Upon these mattresses, covered in sleeping bags, cardboard and anything that might provide any form of warmth were the homeless. It was near inconceivable that anyone could actually live in these conditions, and actually survive them, but they did; the evidence was spread out only too clearly before them. The only saving grace to where they now found themselves was that at least it was out of the driving snow. The Devil had seen many scenes such as this during his time, and it never ceased to sicken him. The knowledge that there was sufficient wealth to supply all these people's needs, and more besides was a lot to bear; it merely lacked the will and the impetus and a universal agreement that something needed to be done. But with the way things were, nothing like that would ever come about, and nothing was ever likely to change. It was the world at large, the world as we knew it.

As they entered the foul-smelling tunnel, a number of those on the mattresses began to stir, some of them even began to sit up, to see who it was out and about at this time of night. Surely the authorities had no intention of moving them on, not so late in the evening - and so near to Christmas too! It was unthinkable.

Roger announced himself to all those present, and straight away the mood began to lighten noticeably. Obviously, some of those present recognised him from previous visits. And they were glad to see him again. As the Devil helped in handing out blankets, it wasn't difficult to see that some of people here were hard drug users, and were in desperate need of help, and that wasn't the sort of help they were disseminating in the form of extra warmth and hot soup. London was awash with people such as this, as was many a city around the world. These were the forgotten multitude, the people that everyone knew existed, but no-one wanted to openly acknowledge. And yet, despite this, there were the good Samaritans still to be had, people such as Roger, Ruth and Dan, all prepared to give of their time in order to distribute what small offerings they had, so as to lighten the burden of those less fortunate than themselves.

Altogether, the four of them spent a good thirty minutes administering to the eight people that sheltered in the underpass, ensuring that if nothing else they at least all had another blanket to ward off the winter chills. After all the hot soup had been consumed, Roger announced that they had to move on; there were other poor souls that needed their help that night, and time was moving inexorably on as it always did.

Slowly, the four of them returned to the van and armed themselves with more of what was left of the blankets and soup. A third trip was out of the question. They would have to manage, somehow. The wind had got up again, and it was even stronger than before, driving the snow relentlessly on. This naturally made the temperature feel even colder than it actually was. As they trudged along, Roger admitted morosely to the Devil.

"This is the part of the evening that always affects us the most. We are like the very large bed and the very small blanket. Whatever we do is never enough. Never near enough. And it's a very sad admission, but it is true."

The Devil said he understood and gave Roger's shoulder a friendly squeeze. "You do what you can," he said, endeavouring to sound upbeat. "This burden is beyond the weight of most people's shoulders; console yourself with that. And remember, no good deed is ever done in vain. Nothing is ever wasted, nor forgotten."

During their second trip, they moved a little further afield and entered what appeared to be a large underground car park. In fact, it was anything but, as Roger went on to explain:

"This concourse was, a few years ago now, where many homeless people used to congregate. It is large, enclosed, and allowed them to bring boxes and belongings here. After a time, it became a permanent residence for many of them. Ultimately it grew and grew and in time became known as 'Cardboard City'. The people who lived here harmed no one, and were a fairly innocuous bunch on the whole. They were simply trying to live their lives to the full, if that's at all possible, in a place like this."

"Then the accident happened," added Dan, glumly.

"What accident was that?" asked the Devil.

"A fire," said Ruth. "And a big one at that. The fire brigade seemed to think one of the homeless down here was possibly using a primus stove that got knocked over. Either way it was never proven, but the outcome was disastrous nevertheless."

"Yes, it was, but those that lived here insisted it was the work of arsonists that wanted to drive them out," said Roger. "Despite the fact that those that occupied this space meant no harm to anyone. In the end everything was cleared out and the local authority boarded everything up, as you can now witness by all the graffiti present."

The Devil looked around, taking it all in.

"And what became of the community that lived here?" he asked.

Roger shook his head unhappily.

"That's the saddest part of the whole escapade. They were all moved on to other places, most of which offered less shelter than did this. It's all rather heart breaking really, after all, they were doing little harm to anyone, and the close kinship that had been formed here was then lost forever. You see, they all looked out for each other, all being in the same boat as the next person. And when someone was ill, everyone knew about it and did what they could to help."

"Makes you wonder if society will ever solve the homeless problem," added Ruth despondently.

Through the next two hours, they were involved in bringing as much comfort to those they encountered as was humanely possible. Eventually, both soup and blankets ran out and they were obliged to return to the van. By now it had gone mid-night and the signs of fatigue were more than evident amongst Roger, Dan and Ruth. The Devil also gave indication of weariness, although he didn't feel it.

Once back at the van, they all piled in and Dan tried to start the engine. It failed to ignite. He tried it again and then again. Each time it failed to turn over. He cursed loudly and banged the steering wheel in his anger and frustration.

"That's all we need! And it will be the same old problem! It always is!" he shouted. "This contraption is falling apart."

"It's just old," said Roger. "Looks like we shall have to walk tonight. We can come back in the morning. I will leave a note on the dash saying we've broken down.

Anyone can see our logo on the side of the van, so they will know it's genuine."

Everyone was about to get out and begin the lengthy walk back to the warehouse, when the Devil announced lightly:

"Don't worry. Let me have a quick look at it. I'm pretty good with engines. Most of the time when something goes wrong the reason is usually pretty mundane. I'm sure it's nothing to worry about. No, you all stay put. No point all of us having to remain out in this weather."

Going on past experience, they all looked most dubious about his well-meaning intentions, and were resigned to having to walk, but there was nothing to lose, so they let him at least try. The Devil asked Dan to raise the bonnet; he then jumped out and then gave the semblance of tinkering with the engine, knocking here, making the odd noise there. As none of the others could see him apparently working beneath the bonnet of the van, they were not party to him actually doing absolutely nothing at all. After a moment or two, he jumped back into the van and suggested that Dan try to start it again. He did so. The engine fired first time, leaving everyone both speechless and very grateful.

"What on earth did you do?" asked Dan in admiration. "This old bone-shaker has been on its way out for the best part of two years now, and I've never heard the engine turn over so smoothly. It's nothing short of a miracle."

The Devil smiled.

"Oh, it was nothing major really, just a little trick I picked up awhile ago. Anyway, shall we go? I'm beginning to feel the affects of a very long day?"

And so off they went. Roger asked him if they could drop him off anywhere, as public transport was a little limited at this time of night. The Devil kindly refused, saying that he had parked up just around the corner from the warehouse.

Having arrived back at their destination in next to no time, all four briefly went inside and Roger thanked the Devil heartily for his sterling efforts. Professing that he had to get home, the Devil then left them to it. As he was leaving, he casually touched the side of the large van, allowing a certain enchantment to unfold. Not that anyone saw him of course.

"Nothing quite like a little latent good will," he mused with a smile.

After word

The following day, Roger, Dan and Ruth met up in the afternoon back at the warehouse, with a view to getting themselves organised and readied for the evening ahead. Dan, whose job it was to look after the van, was altogether flabbergasted when he left his house that morning, only to find that the van had quite dramatically changed over night. And it was some transformation. For some unknown reason, he found, instead of the old battered vehicle he was used to, a brand new one that shone brightly like a new pin. He looked at it aghast and utterly mystified. It made little or no sense to him at all. The key he had on his fob fitted perfectly in the lock, the number plate was the same, as it ever was, and the logo on the side of the van was the same, too. What on earth had taken place overnight? Exactly what, was going on here?

Having finally accepted his near disbelief at what had happened to the van, he drove it to the warehouse, unsure of how he was going to explain it to the others. When he arrived, he was altogether surprised to find both Roger and Ruth standing at the entrance to the warehouse, both looking equally bemused. Upon seeing him, they beckoned him over. What he saw took his breath away and left him all agog for the second time that morning. The warehouse was veritably filled to the rafters with all manner of things: blankets, coats, hats, gloves, scarves, sleeping bags, large tins of soup, additional thermos flasks. But where had it all come from? None of them had an answer to that question, not so much as a clue. As they stood trying to take it all in, they were approached by two young men, who asked for Roger. They introduced themselves and said that they had both been employed, and paid well in advance, to help out that evening. Neither was sure who had been responsible for it, but they weren't unduly bothered by that. Roger was only too glad of the extra help. He rang the office to see if they could throw any further light on everything that had taken place. As might be expected to learn, they couldn't.

A Match Made in Heaven

Being the 22nd December a.m.

With a desire to make an early start, the Devil was in Leicester Square promptly that morning. If the anecdotal bird of note had but kept to its usual temporal and timely routine, then it would, on this particular morning, already have found the worm well and truly conspicuous by its absence. A thick crusting of snow had fallen during the night, making a white blanket everywhere and causing treachery underfoot; but the Devil was up and about his rounds, knowing that a timely start was imperative if he was to achieve his desire and fulfil his agenda that day. Yes, he most definitely had an agenda: it had been long planned out, and thoroughly committed to memory; but, even so, despite his being a stickler for routine, and being utterly opposed to change, he often recognised a certain rebelliousness in his own nature – a certain call to recklessness if you will – and an utter opposition to the asperity of his usual rigid and orderly way of doing things. Yes, common sense does tell us that black is black and white is white, but that being the case there were, if truth be told, many different shades in between, and each and every one of them had a calling all of their own. And that being the case, who was he to ignore any one of them?

The sun was up, the sky was an azure blue, there was not a cloud to be seen anywhere – but my, oh my, the temperature was low that morning; so low in fact as to make the burning sun seem insincere in its exploits, as it winged its way merrily across the firmament, displaying its fiery effulgence to the world. Banging his hands together as a sign that he was more than ready to take on anything that the world could throw at him, he pressed on. It was now exactly eight a.m. and Trafalgar Square was looking pretty empty, as most people currently on their way to work tended to circumvent it. The only one's present were stall holders, who were situated near the far end by the National Gallery, and they were busily readying themselves for the annual festive consumer onslaught. There were a total number of sixteen stalls in all, every one of them built to the same Bavarian chalet style – but there the similarity ended. Each of them sold items as diverse as Christmas ornaments, ornate picture frames, hand knitted scarves and hats, children's toys – and not to mention a dubious alcoholic beverage of nameless origin that promised to fulfil all seasonal expectations - whatever that was supposed to mean. All the stalls looked complete and thoroughly geared up for the Christmas shoppers, that would very soon descend upon them in their hundreds.

As the Devil entered the Square, his eye was drawn towards a young man who was engaged in removing the newly fallen snow from the steps. It looked an arduous task for one person, and judging by the expression on the young man's face, he was in whole agreement with that sentiment. He looked utterly dejected and completely miserable in the extreme. Despite it being well below zero, sweat was running in streams down his face. It appeared as though his very existence depended upon finishing clearing the steps of snow in double quick time, and he was endeavouring to overtake what was expected of him.

Watching him briefly, the Devil couldn't help but feel sorry for the young man; looking so heavily laden, with what appeared to be more than the present task in hand. He thought that it was time for a little intervention. Crossing the Square, in a hop, skip and a jump of ebullience, he called out to him.

"A Merry Christmas to you, my young friend! My, oh my, that looks pretty gruelling work if you ask me. It does indeed!"

For the briefest of seconds, but only the very briefest mind, the young man looked up from what he was doing; but even so, during that time he never slowed in his pursuits for an instant, and replied:

"Yes, it is." And then quickly returned to his task.

There was no Christmas cheer, or festive merriment about the young man, absolutely none whatsoever; and that saddened the Devil immensely. It was almost as if many years previous, some self-centred person had told him that Christmas amounted to very little in real terms, and was in fact a complete and utter waste of everyone's time – and he had firmly believed it then and was now continuing with that self-same belief. It was as though, all that was seemingly left to him, was a grey backdrop of ceaseless people running hither and thither and making themselves a slave to a tradition, without any real meaning to it all. Things had to change. And he would make sure that they did.

Looking intently at the young man, and the way he seemed without any great purpose, the Devil couldn't help but feel an intense pity for him, a pity born of knowing better, and knowing it in his heart too, and what's more to the very core of his being. And this being the case, he felt that it behooved him to change the young man's mind about Christmas, and everything that it stood for. It now became his life's work.

"You certainly look to me as though you could do with a little help," the Devil said cheerfully.

Believing that the man was doing his level best to mock him, the young man replied in a somewhat and rather irritable manner.

"If you're offering to help, there's a spare broom just over there, right next to my trolley. Feel free to use it. Please do. No-one else will be using it."

No sooner had the words issued forth from the young man's mouth and the Devil had said broom in his hand. He began cleaning snow from the steps as though there was no tomorrow, causing the young man to look on in mystified awe and amazement. He also noted, that despite his youth, there was no way he could keep up a similar pace with what the Devil was now exhibiting. The man was a veritable blur; he seemed possessed, and snow was sent skittering from the steps in all directions. Was the man on drugs or some such?

"Er, thanks," was all he could think of to say. But then, what could he say? Who was this guy, coming out of nowhere like he did? What were his intentions?

In what appeared to be no time at all, every step was glistening again and devoid of all the wintry white stuff, and what is more, the Devil didn't seem any the worse for his efforts. He was now standing on the foremost step, grinning broadly, as though he were the King of the Castle, having valiantly vanquished all the offending snow that had dared to affront him.

"There," he said with near smug satisfaction. "That didn't take any time at all now, did it? What's your name by the way, I'm Nick?"

"Er, Terry," replied the young man, looking and sounding most uncomfortable with the situation. "Thank you once again, but I've got to salt the steps now - It's to stop people from slipping, you see - We don't want them suing the council. And it does happen, you know. Again, thanks for all your help, I really appreciate it. I won't keep you."

"But the job is only half completed," said the Devil, exhibiting near overwhelming exuberance. "I can't leave you to do all that on your own as well now, can I? It wouldn't be very charitable of me, would it? This being Christmas, and all. That would never do."

The situation was beginning to make Terry feel a little more uncomfortable than he was used to.

"You really don't have to," he said. "I'm sure you have other more pressing things to do. It is Christmas after all, as you've just pointed out. I don't wish to keep you from it."

Maintaining a sublime bearing throughout, the Devil replied:

"Yes, it is true, Terry, I do have much to do – but if I can't take a few minutes out of my schedule to help a fellow passenger on life's long and perilous route to the afterlife, then I believe it reflects badly upon me. And anyway, I've told you, it really is no bother at all. A pleasure, in fact. And I feel sure, between the two of us, we should get this job completed in next to no time – now, where do you keep that salt?"

Finding the man's willingness to openly partake in his own drudgery and labour was all rather embarrassing and altogether mystifying at the same time. But, as he was so insistent, and what's more appeared to be genuinely interested in helping, he felt he could not argue the point.

And so they began, like two old chums, setting about their task with a vigour. How they managed to finish it in what appeared to be double-quick time, Terry couldn't quite fathom, but they did, nevertheless.

Having finally completed the job of distributing salt, Terry once again thanked this kind-hearted passer-by – (he was now beginning to change his opinion of him), and said that he had to tidy everything away and report back to the depot. Before he left, the Devil shook him warmly by the hand and wished him a very merry Christmas. Terry did likewise. It was odd, he thought to himself, generally this time of year usually left him feeling cold, and yet for some odd reason this perfect stranger was making him see things in a wholly new light. No doubt it would pass and things would revert to normal, once again soon.

The Devil took his leave, allowing Terry the fairly simple job of putting everything away. Making his way towards the small Bavarian type huts, he could see that most of them were now doing a brisk business, which was to be expected. Genial folk came and went, most of them loaded down with gifts that they had just purchased; others were merely strolling and taking in the atmosphere and the wonderful treats that were on offer; not actually buying, but appreciating what was available anyway. The feeling of good-will was perceptible and fairly added a universal warmth to the chilly morning.

Every stall that the Devil passed had something new to offer, though he was making for one stall in particular – and there it was, tucked away, slightly to one side. He stopped and read the sign that adorned the front: *'J.Bergdahl – Seller of Hand-Crafted Knitted Goods'* The wealth of colour and vibrancy that met him from the stall was as near too overwhelming as you could imagine. A veritable cornucopia of different shades of the brightest wools and materials conceivable: there were hats, scarves, woollen mittens, body warmers, socks and a host of other things, all hand made, and all ready to be donned to keep out the winter cold and chills.

Having just supplied a customer with a full regalia of woollen multi-coloured protection against the winter weather, the young woman settled herself down on a folding chair, took up some knitting and began the process of producing yet another item for sale. The Devil did not speak, but watched her with eager interest. At last, she looked up from what she was doing and caught his eye.

"Hello," she said, gaily. "Can I help you?"

Her tone was vibrant and positive, and she appeared to bubble over with such effusive charm and goodwill he found that it was enough to fair take your breath away. Her natural upbeat exuberance was as close to being physical as you could imagine. The Devil couldn't help but think that if it were possible to connect her smile and vivacity to the national grid then the debt crisis would be over in the blink of an eye, and the country would be back in the black again.

"I was just looking at your sign," he said, pointing to it. "Bergdahl – that's an unusual name - Scandinavian, isn't it? And what's the J for – no, let me guess – Jota? No, that's not it – er, Jennine, perhaps?"

"It's stands for Johanna, but my friends call me Jo-Jo," she said, cutting short his thought processes.

"Ah, Jo-Jo, is it? A particularly nice name, I think. Your merchandise is certainly most colourful may I say? It draws the eye and no mistake. I see according to your sign that it is all handmade. It seems an awful lot of work just for one person if you don't mind my observing."

The young woman laughed loudly, and it was laugh that might have lifted anyone's gloom and raised their spirits to the very highest level had they heard it.

"Why, bless you," she said. "No, if I had to do all this by myself then it would have taken me in excess of a year! I've a mother and two willing aunt's who help me enormously. They are knitting constantly, just to keep up with demand. And what with it being Christmas. It's gone crazy mad, it really has."

She laughed again and the Devil joined in with her.

"Why, yes, of course, how stupid of me not to realise something as obvious as that. So, business is rather good then?"

Jo-Jo nodded.

"Oh yes. It's even better than I could ever have hoped for, but I'm not complaining. It certainly keeps me busy. Not always easy to keep up with demand though. I think I need a manager, or someone with experience in business studies just to help me keep on top of things."

"By the sound of it, it certainly sounds like you need a little extra help."

She smiled.

"Well, I suppose if I had someone to help with the paperwork and the finance, and one or two other things, then it would certainly relieve me of a few things and I could deal more effectively with the stock side of the company. One of the hazards of being self-employed and running your own business. It's certainly been a learning curve."

"Do I detect a certain south-American influence with the items you produce here?" he asked, picking up a sweater and appearing to examine it more closely.

"Why, yes, you do. I suppose the bright colours do give it away a bit,' she replied. "I was originally born in Mexico, but my parents emigrated to Sweden when I was a child and then I came to London later. I do go back to my homeland every once in a while. In fact, I travelled there extensively a few years back now, back-packing with a few friends and what not. I've always found the bright natural colours and designs of the clothing that the locals wore gave the impression that they must be of a happy disposition; and in truth they were. Then, when I returned home, I thought what a great idea it would be to reproduce what I had seen and see if there was a market for it here."

"Well, it has to be said that you certainly appear to have found a fairly lucrative outlet for what you make. And, if I may say so, it appears to be of very good quality too. Which brings me on to why I stopped to peruse your merchandise to begin with. Let me explain. You see, I have four nieces; and to be honest I can never think of what to buy them for Christmas. It's a constant nightmare. Absolutely dread this time of year. There's no-one worse than I for not being able to get the present situation just right. And I rarely do. I believe I must be the world's worst. But looking at what you have here, I think it may be the answer to my problem."

He then went on to relate the ages of his nieces, how they were all very different in their tastes, exactly what colours they liked; it seemed without end.

"They are all very loud and highly opinionated," he said, continuing with his narrative. "I believe most youngsters are like that nowadays. It's difficult to know what they like, though I do know bright colours are top of the list. I think if I opt for four hats, four scarves and four sets of gloves then I should become their favourite uncle again. Oh, and if you could possibly make it the hats with the flaps on either side; you know, those ones that come down and cover the ears; those with the tassels on – yes, that would be marvellous. They will go down an absolute storm. Many thanks."

Jo-Jo sorted out precisely what he wanted and placed them into two carrier bags. She then totted up the cost of his purchases and asked him:

"How would you prefer to pay, cash or card?"

"Oh, cash, most definitely," he replied. "Always cash. I've always had a loathing for gadgets and contraptions and all those modern ways of doing things. In my opinion there's nothing quite so reliable and unpretentious as good old-fashioned currency. You always know where you are with it. And I do not believe it will ever go out of fashion – at least not if I have anything to do with it."

As he finished speaking, and almost as if it had been fated, part of the counter appeared to suddenly give way, allowing most of the merchandise to slide inexorably to the one end of the stall. Jo-Jo managed to prevent it all from cascading to the floor, and the Devil also did his bit to help with the rescue.

"It's never done that before," she observed, becoming most put out by what had happened. "It must have developed a fault or something. I don't know what I'm going to do now, I really don't."

The Devil was totally effusive in his sympathy with her plight and pointed out that there must be a management team on hand to address such things as this. Jo-Jo admitted that she did have a number to call, should any eventuality like this arise, but she never envisaged having to use it.

"Excellent," said the Devil, and offered to hold the counter up while she did the necessaries and ring for help.

Jo-Jo rang the number she had and kept it ringing for what appeared to be ages, but ultimately no-one picked up and the phone eventually cut out. She tried calling several times, but was met with the same. After this she had no idea as to what to do next and began to deliberate as to whether she should just pack up for the day and return home, despite only recently having started trading. The prospect did not fill her with much joy. The Devil then offered a possible solution to her problem.

"You know, a very good friend of mine just happens to be working very close by here," he said. "He's a dab hand at this sort of thing – very practically minded. In fact, he's an absolute wizard if I'm honest. Me, I'm hopeless at anything like this; totally useless, but I have no doubt he will be able to fix it in a jiffy. Will you be all right to hold the fort a few moments while I go and get him? It shouldn't take long."

Jo-Jo said she would manage, leaving the Devil to go off in search of a much-needed ally, who could help in a crisis.

Terry, whom the Devil had helped earlier with the snow clearance and the salting, was in the process of just putting away his last few items; he was feeling pretty upbeat about things, all things considered; he had finished earlier than planned, all thanks to Nick, and was now off to grab a well-deserved hot coffee, and not to mention a bit of a thaw out, and possibly a doughnut as well. The prospect of such simple pleasures filled him with a satisfying glow. Then, as he looked up, he saw none other than the man from earlier making his way towards him, and all the while throwing his arms about and gesticulating wildly in an apparent attempt to get his attention. As he drew nearer, looking for all the world as though he was an octopus throwing a fit, Terry wondered what on the earth could be the problem,

"What is it?" he asked. "I'm finished for a bit and I need to go and get hold of a hot drink."

"That will have to wait awhile," said the Devil, with great urgency and stipulation that warranted no objection at all. "I need your help – or, to be more precise – a certain young lady, just across the way there, needs your help. It's an absolute emergency."

"What young lady? Can't you deal with it? I've just told you; I need to get a drink and warm up a bit, I'm absolutely freezing! I can't feel my fingers."

"Nonsense!" returned the Devil. "Young chap like you, a little chilly weather like this – it's bracing. And I will happily stand you to a hot mug of something if you will just come and help out. It won't take more than two minutes, I promise. And you will be doing someone a very good turn – it is Christmas, after all; the time for doing good deeds and what not; a bit of festive spirit as they say, or are you objecting to that?"

Terry didn't feel as though he could refuse such a request, especially considering how helpful the man had been earlier. Realising how futile it would be to argue with him, he followed meekly after him, though he had a certain modicum of resentment brewing in his breast as he did so. Whatever the problem was, hopefully it wouldn't take too long to sort out, and then he could get about his business and have a hot drink.

Once they had returned to where Jo-Jo was still stoically holding up the one end of the counter-top, whilst trying to deal with a customer at the same time, the Devil announced chivalrously:

"Jo-Jo, this is Terry. He's a top-notch handyman, absolutely first class, and he has agreed, as a big favour to me, to see what the problem is. Now, I know that it makes me look a bit of a party-pooper, especially with an emergency such as this unravelling about our ears, but I really have to fly. You see, I have an appointment booked, and I cannot afford to be late for it, so I am going to have to love and leave you both. Is it all right if I call back later for my items, only as you will appreciate, I can't very well go into a business meeting lugging two bags full of woollens now, can I? Don't worry, I won't be more than an hour or two at most. I'll see you later – Bye!"

And with that he was gone in an instant, leaving a very mystified Terry and Jo-Jo watching him quickly disappear up the Charing Cross Road.

"Well," said Jo-Jo with a grin, "Your friend is certainly a little unique, isn't he?"

Turning to face her, a very puzzled looking Terry replied.

"He's no friend of mine. I don't know the man from Adam. I've never met him before this morning. I was just cleaning the steps and he suddenly appeared out of nowhere, grabs a broom and starts to help. It was really weird. In fact, he's weird. Oddest man I've ever met, if I was honest. There's something about him that I can't quite put my finger on."

"Well, odd or not, he certainly appears to know you. If he didn't, how would he know that you are a good handyman?"

A look of puzzlement crossed Terry's face.

"A handyman? I'm not a handyman. I'm the least handy person you could ever wish to meet. I have trouble tying my shoe-laces. Why on earth would he tell you that?"

Jo-Jo shook her head, utterly mystified by it all.

"I really have no idea," she said. "But I do know that this counter is very heavy and I don't think I can hold it up for much longer."

This was the cue for Terry to finally intervene, which he did so only too readily, despite the fact that he had no idea precisely what was going on, or what this 'Nick's' game was all about. Taking the weight of the counter, he looked beneath to see if anything was obviously amiss. It was true, he was no handyman, and he would be the first to admit it, but if he could help at all then he was only too happy to do so. After a few seconds of searching for the problem, he could be heard to exclaim triumphantly.

"I've found it!" Letting go of the counter top, it became apparent that all was now well. "All fixed." he added confidently.

Jo-Jo looked on in admiration. "For someone who professes not to be a handyman, you sure are handy," she said. "That's great! You've really saved my bacon. What was the problem?"

"Oh, it was nothing major. There's a bolt just underneath there that secures the counter in place. For some odd reason it had come loose. I'm not really sure how, as it has a safety catch on it which should have prevented that sort of thing from happening. It's really odd. It's as if someone had purposefully taken the catch off so it could work its way loose. But that doesn't make any sense, does it?"

"Ah, I suppose it's just one of those things that happens from time to time," said Jo-Jo dismissively and then grinned. "Either way, you've saved me having to pack up and go home early, and, what's more, lose a whole day's sales as well. Which I can't afford to do at Christmas. How much do I owe you for your time?"

Terry looked horrified at the notion of getting paid for something that had taken him no time at all to sort out, and promptly said so.

"You don't owe me anything," he explained. "Glad I could be of help. Anyhow, I must be off. I've promised myself a hot drink before I report back to the depot. I'll let you get back to your selling. Pretty nice stuff you have here by the way. It looks classy – and warm too."

Jo-Jo thanked him and smiled a truly disarming smile that made him wish that he didn't have to go.

"I've got a large thermos of hot chocolate, if you'd like some," she said. "I have two cups, and it's the least I can do, considering how helpful you have been. Please say you will have a cup with me."

She smiled again. Terry smiled back. He liked this girl. There was something strangely familiar about her, though he couldn't have said why. It was as if he had known her for years. And what was more she made him feel good.

From across the road, and well obscured, so as not to be seen by either of them, the Devil watched the pair with a rising smile. His work here was now complete. It was going to be a match made in heaven. And there was no doubt about it.

After word

Terry and Jo-Jo hit it off right from the start, just as the Devil had prophesised they would. Terry stayed awhile, had his hot chocolate, and before he was obliged to return to his depot, asked if he could see Jo-Jo again. She liked him, and felt a connection, and was only too happy to oblige. She learnt, in time, that Terry had a degree in Business Studies: the principles of business, management and economics came in very handy in the running and expanding of her business. In time, Terry, gave up working for the local authority and the two formed a partnership. This was a precursor to a very successful business. The question arose as to why Terry, having such a useful qualification, that should have set him up for a successful career, would spend his time with a broom, sweeping the streets. Well, the truth being told, he felt he hadn't found his true calling in life and was waiting for something more unequivocal and undeniable to enter his existence. After meeting Jo-Jo, it had to be said this is precisely what happened. Or, as the Devil put it, it was a match made in heaven.

Spiv

Being still the 22nd December

As he made his way up the Charing Cross Road, taking his time as he went, a fine sprinkling of snow began to fall; though the Devil knew it wouldn't cause Terry any major problems. He hadn't travelled very far, when his gaze fell upon the second object of his intentions that day: a huge burly individual, standing in excess of six feet tall and nearly as wide. The man, appeared to be in his fifties and had gnarled, scarred facial features that carried the evidence of every blow he had ever received. Viewing the man's hands, which were so large and knobby, the Devil could see that they could easily have graced the arms of any Neanderthal. As he continued to watch the man, he could see that he seemed totally absorbed in focusing his entire attention on the opposite side of the street, where a small crowd had gathered around a young gentleman, who appeared to be in the process of selling items, from what looked like a large suitcase of some description. The Devil slowly approached the larger man and smiled in a friendly fashion. The man, in his turn, caught the gesture out of the corner of his eye and promptly ignored it, not allowing his attention to waiver even for an instant from what was going on over the other side of the street. The Devil then spoke, reciting a poem that he was familiar with.

'It was today upon the stair

I met a man who wasn't there

He wasn't there again today

O' how I wish he'd go away.'

The brawny individual stopped his observations, and looking extremely uncomprehending, turned in the Devil's direction.

"What?" he barked aggressively, though not sufficiently enough to draw undue attention to himself from the passing shoppers.

The Devil went on to explain.

"That was a little ditty from O'Henry, aka William Sydney Porter," he replied. "It has always amused me. I thought I would introduce a little levity into the proceedings, here. Not a great fan? Well, never mind. Let's put this one down to the one that got away, eh?"

The man now looked totally confused, and leant towards the Devil in a very threatening manner.

"I don't know what your game is, sunshine, but take some good advice from me and clear off, and be quick about it – or else you'll regret it! You got it?"

Not one to allow himself to be cow-towed, by either verbal abuse or threats of physical violence, the Devil did nothing of the sort, and therefore remained exactly where he was. He did, however, avert his gaze to take in the other man across the street, taking particular notice of what he was doing. The man was far younger than his hefty colleague, and it was apparent that he was the undoubted 'brains' of the outfit. At that precise moment, he appeared to be doing a rather brisk trade in defrauding the public, by selling them ingenuous bottles of what appeared to be fragrances of some description, all nicely boxed and all looking highly authentic. He was calling out to the passers-by, advertising cut price original goods. This was obviously false, as could be attested to by the presence of the Neanderthal, who's job it was to look out for trouble, namely in the form of the local constabulary. A definite spiv, if I ever saw one, thought the Devil to himself. And he had seen a few in his time.

"None of it is genuine, of course," he remarked loudly to the hulking behemoth at his side. This caused the man to cast an even more menacing eye upon him than before. Taking hold of the Devil's shoulder and gripping it with a hand that would have done justice to a sasquatch, he said:

"I've told you once! Now, I'm not going to tell you again – clear orf! Got it?"

"I hate to point out the obvious my brawny pugilist, but you rather just did, didn't you, tell me twice, I mean? Bit of a non-sequitur, wouldn't you agree? Or may be in your case, not."

The brute had no idea what the Devil was talking about, but was convinced, at the very least, that he was trying to make a fool of him. This was something the Devil was often being accused of, and in many instances, it was perfectly true. He took hold of the Devil's shoulder, and began to squeeze it rather hard, just to show that he meant business. Any normal person would have, by now, been squirming in a paroxysm of pain and agony, but then the Devil, understandably, did not fall into this particular category. Instead, he merely smiled blissfully and said, without any trace of malice:

"My, my, you really don't look well at all, do you? I shouldn't wonder if you aren't coming down with something rather unpleasant. So many nasty things doing the rounds now, don't you know? Bugs, germs, viruses and what not. Nasty little blighters."

As soon as the Devil had uttered these portentous words, the Neanderthal did indeed begin to look decidedly unwell. His pallor turned an odd greenish shade and he looked for all the world as though he was about to pass out.

"Here, let me lend a hand, as I can see you are not having a good time of things at all," said the Devil, and taking hold of his arm began leading him towards a nearby bench. "Now, you take my advice and remain here for a while, and in next to no time you will be feeling as right as rain again. I can virtually guarantee it."

The man could do little else. It was true, he felt as weak as a kitten, and a rather, small sickly one at that. All he needed was a few minutes to get his breath back and he would be fine again (or so he told himself). And, as he sat there, doing his level best to recover his strength and wits a little, it occurred to him, that perhaps it was time to find some other form of employment; something altogether less stressful and demanding of him. In the coming weeks he would certainly give the matter some serious thought.

Feeling full of good humour, and having dispensed with the ogre, without having to resort to anything other than suggestion, the Devil left the man perched precariously on the bench, leaving the general public to ruminate as to how anyone could allow themselves to get into such a pitiful state so early in the morning, it being the festive season, or not, and tripped lightly across the road, avoiding the on-coming traffic with the dexterity of a ballet-dancer.

Unaware that his watch-out had been suitably rendered hors-de-combat, the younger man was enthusiastically and erstwhile engaged in selling his crude reproductions to the fairly large and altogether unwary crowd that had now gathered around him. It never ceased to amaze the Devil just how easy it was to fool people, especially when a bargain seemed to be at the centre of it. Picking up a sampler bottle, the Devil smelled its contents, before replacing it.

"Altogether fraudulent, and rather obvious, too," he announced, loud enough for everyone in the vicinity to hear him.

The young man, having just finished serving another apparently happy customer, who had purchased two bottles of perfume, plus a bottle of after-shave, looked up and cast the Devil an altogether withering look, that he straightaway ignored.

"This is all kosher, my friend," he said, doing his best to look and sound amiable. "There's no rubbish here. It's all bankrupt stock. Every bit of it. That's how I can sell it so cheap; everyone gets a bargain, and nobody loses out. See? It's all pretty simple."

The Devil made a great display of tutting loudly, which also got everyone's attention, much to the annoyance of the young man.

"That really isn't the truth now, is it?" he said. "Remember the old axiom, tell the truth and shame the devil. Well, it may be better to do that long term, and by so doing you wouldn't be taking advantage of these poor people and depriving them of all their hard-earned money, now would you?"

"What do you mean by that?" asked the man, with rising anger. "You've smelled the goods – it's all genuine! I defy anyone here to take these tester bottles, have them analysed and then tell me that they aren't all the genuine article."

"Oh, I agree," said the Devil. "What you say is perfectly true. Every tester you have laid out here does indeed contain the genuine article; it's just unfortunate that the same cannot be said for what you are selling here amongst the other items you have laid out. This is all mass produced in a small warehouse in Bermondsey. In short – it's total and utter junk, and you're conning everyone here. Shame on you, sir. You should be ashamed of yourself. And it being Christmas too."

To say that the man was not now party to such a shock that it caused his jaw to drop, would have been a gross miss-truth; and the truth can sometimes do this, when it is revealed in all its stark and hideous glory. The man's brain, shocked into some form of response, took the route from neutral to first gear - he blathered, spluttered a little, and then managed to compose himself sufficiently, at least, to say:

"And I suppose you have some kind of proof to back that up, do you? No, I thought not. So, clear off. You're embarrassing yourself."

The Devil smiled again and then nodded, good-naturedly. Always one to rise to a challenge, he placed his hand inside his pocket and quickly took out a series of high-resolution photographs. Some of the customers now became very interested in the proceedings and began to barge one another to get a better look.

"A word to the wise," said the Devil to the young man. "It never pays to kid a kidder – and never, ever, gamble unless you have a winning hand. Now, what do we have here? This particular photograph shows you outside the factory…. And this one clearly shows you liaising with your colleagues inside the factory, and also shows the actual process of the manufacture of your illicit merchandise….and this particular one - such a great close-up, don't you think? shows you helping to load said merchandise into your van. I think I rest my case here, yes?"

An ominous silence descended upon the crowd. All those customers who had heard what had been going on, now began to take quite an interest in the young man, who, in turn, now began to look more like a trapped animal with each passing second. Voices became decidedly raised, causing the man to go on the defensive; he felt confident that if he did so, then he could soon overcome any dissatisfaction with pure brute intransigence. It had worked before, on more than one occasion, and surely it would work again   He began to become most insistent that he never made refunds, regardless of the circumstances, and that the onus was upon the buyer - caveat emptor being the only bit of Latin that he knew. The small crowd that had gathered about him, upon hearing this, were not altogether happy with the response, which in turn caused something approaching bedlam to break out. Everyone wanted their money returned. This universal demand was then suitably enforced by one large, altogether aggressive gentleman, who having purchased two bottles of the fragrances on offer, one for his wife and the other for his daughter, and who was now feeling decidedly cheated, grabbed the younger man by the front of his jacket and physically hauled him up over the front of the small table that contained the remainder of the goods. This was quickly followed by a demand for his money to be returned in full, along with everyone else's, and a severe intimation of what dire consequences would ensue if it wasn't. A look of panic crossed the young man's features. He looked around for sign of the Neanderthal, but seeing no-one, realized that the game was well and truly up for him.

The Devil stood quietly by watching the proceedings with a certain smug satisfaction. Justice was playing itself out, which it invariably did when he was involved.

Then, giving the impression that he didn't wish to upset anyone, especially at this festive time of the year, the young man offered to refund any money in full. The noise and anger slowly abated as he slowly began to dispense the necessaries. People accepted what was owed them and then slowly began moving away. Very soon only the young man, the Devil and the large gentleman were left. The gentleman had purposefully chosen to remain last to be served in order to ensure that everyone was rightfully given their due. Had he not, he felt there was a distinct possibility the man might renege on his promise and not return everyone's money. Once he had received what was owed to him, and just for good measure and to put a final seal on proceedings, the large man punched the younger one in the eye, making him fall to the floor; he then turned and left, leaving just the two of them alone.

Lying prostrate amongst the brown churned up snow, that lay in large slushy heaps in the alleyway, the young man nursed his wounded pride, but particularly his bruised eye, which was beginning to swell noticeably. Taking hold of the young man's arm, the Devil slowly helped him to his feet.

"You got off pretty lightly, I think, all told, don't you?" he mused.

The young man failed to follow the Devil's reasoning, and quickly made his point known.

"I don't know how you make that out!" he said, angrily. "And where the bleeding hell has Ronnie got to? I pay that lazy sod to prevent this sort of thing from happening?"

The Devil made a casual gesture towards the other side of the street.

"Your pugilistic friend across the way there was suddenly taken rather unwell, I believe. I think it's quite possible that he has gone down with something. So many nasty things going around, especially at this time of year. I said as much to him myself, not so long ago. Either way, I do believe he has now returned home. A change of heart perhaps? Who knows? Not that it matters. I firmly believe he won't be pugilising anyone for a long time to come. Changing tack, but briefly, I used to be a bit of a fan of the old bare-knuckle fisticuff thing myself many years ago – not actually participating you understand – no, more of an interested casual observer: Tom Cribb, Tom Johnson, Jem Belcher. Great fighters they were. I saw them all. And not forgetting good old Henry Pierce – known as the Game Chicken, he was. He could take a man out with either hand, and so very often did. Never beaten. Extraordinary. Ah, halcyon times, don't you know? Old Jem lost an eye. Very sad business. I warned him not to play racket-ball. It will end in tears, I said. It will end in tears. But people rarely listen to sound advice, in my experience. Let me ask you, Michael, are you the sort of person to listen to sound advice, especially when it is given in good faith?"

The young man eyed the Devil suspiciously, having every reason to do so, especially in light of what had just happened to him.

"How come you know my name?" he asked, suspiciously. "You a private investigator, or something?"

"I know your name the same way I know of your unsalutary goings on in Bermondsey," replied the Devil. "But that really isn't important now. What is important is what you choose to do at this point in your life. I can assure you that your very future depends on it."

There was a perceptible hint of menace in the way the Devil spoke, which caused Michael to pause slightly before responding.

"…Well, Mr Nosey-Parker, I will tell you exactly what I intend to do – not that it's any of your damn business, anyway. And the only reason I am going to tell you is I want to see the expression on your superior face when I do. How you managed to get hold of those photos and pull that stunt just now I have no idea. But I will tell you this, once I leave here, I intend to return to where I got this lot, restock and come straight back. And when I do, I shall return to another part of the city, where you can't find me – oh, and I shall be bringing along a couple of colleagues, who won't take too kindly to seeing your ugly face around – That's if you catch my drift. I hope I've made myself plain."

The Devil looked Michael straight in the eye, giving him an intense, piercing look, and asked him:

"Are you sure you won't reconsider? Change your mind, perhaps? Give a little Christmas thought to those that you intend to defraud and rob? It's a sure sign of altruism and philanthropy, and what is more an earnest desire to turn over a new leaf. And you can't even begin to imagine how far it goes towards redeeming your soul."

Michael made a noise of contempt and returned to gathering up the goods which had fallen to the floor. The small table, being of a clever design, and which doubled as a large suitcase, allowed him to collect everything together in next to no time. He then made to leave, only to find that the Devil was blocking his way.

"I see that my words of advice, though given in all honest benevolence, have fallen upon deaf ears," he said, sadly. "What a great pity, what a great, great pity, Michael. Ah, the unsavoury nature of man – and his unwillingness to conform, even when faced with impending disaster. It never ceases to amaze, it really doesn't. Then, so be it. You have made your decision, despite my counselling. Therefore, it behooves me to inform you that your lesson will now commence."

Quickly taking Michael's arm, he gazed deeply into his eyes, his own, now blazing a fierce intense red, much like an inferno erupting from the inner workings of an exploding volcano.

"Look upon me, Michael and view what awaits you should you fail to give up your unwholesome and wicked ways. You are a reprehensible and loathsome human being and your fate is now cemented by your actions, and not least by the choices you make."

As the Devil spoke, the colour began to drain away from Michael's face. His eyes glazed over perceptibly and his expression became vacuous, empty, unseeing; but that merely hid what was taking place within him. He began to witness things that no mortal man should ever witness, and he became aware that, up until that moment he hadn't been aware of, that he had in fact a soul; but having witnessed it he saw that it was stunted and blackened, and that it carried a gut-wrenching fetid miasma about it that issued forth from it that made him want to vomit. This vision seemed to last an age – but was in reality little more than a few seconds of earthly time. Then all at once the vision ended, he was left with a sharp, intense pain that he did not know the origin of. It affected his whole body, and was excruciating to say the least. He heard a voice that appeared to drift towards him through the ether.

"Pull out of it!" it called. The Devil then gave him another healthy slap across the face that nearly took him off his feet.

"Wh – What?" said Michael, then placed his hands across his face in abject terror, fully recalling what he had just seen. "Oh, dear God! What was that? What was it?"

The Devil smiled and gave him a hearty slap on the back.

"Why, that was opportunity, Michael. And also, a foretaste, if you will, of what may be. But don't take it so much to heart. Though I advise you to take my word for it when I say, you really do not want to return to your old perfidious ways. If you do then you may find yourself fully consigned to what you witnessed. I tell you what, how about I give you a copy of the graphic novel of what you have just beheld, just as a reminder – let's call it an early Christmas present? No? Well, if, you're sure. It was just a thought."

As the Devil watched him, Michael became very animated - but then, having observed what he had just witnessed it was hardly surprising. It wasn't at all unusual for people to expire on the spot, having seen what Michael had observed in his vision. But he took no notice of that. Spurred on by what he now needed to do, he began taking up the boxes of perfume and started removing the cellophane wrapping. He worked like a man possessed in his efforts. The Devil watched him, totally fascinated by it all.

"Michael, what precisely are you doing?" he asked.

"Got to tip all this stuff away!" he replied in a frenzy. "It's not legit! None of it is! I've got to – It has to go - I've got to get rid of it!"

Laying a pacifying hand upon his arm, the Devil said soothingly:

"I have a much better idea, Michael. Why don't you simply give it all away to worthy causes? Naturally, you will be required to tell them the truth about it, that being that none of it is the genuine article; but even so, by doing that you may go some way to absolving yourself of blame – and of course, you will also make a lot of people very happy in the process. Now, how does that sound?"

Michael straight away took the idea on board; he got his thinking straight, and agreed that it was an excellent idea.

"Yes, yes, that's a good thing to do – I'll do that – Yes, I'll do that…" he said absently, repacking the bottles and the boxes.

The Devil continued to watch him as he drifted away down the small alley-way towards Soho and China Town. He wasn't worried at all by the thought of Michael relapsing and reverting to his old ways. The lesson he had learnt that day would never leave him. It was job well done. Clapping his hands together in satisfaction, being his customary way, he headed off towards a small, quaint, coffee shop right near Leicester Square tube station. The beverages were always good there, and they also sold the most delicious French fancies, which he had always had a particular weakness for.

The script was already written, he knew that only too well – but from time to time, it was great fun just to tweak at the edges – just a little bit, that is.

After word

Ronnie did indeed retire after his encounter with the Devil. Time, he felt, had finally caught up with him. 'It was a mugs game' he remarked to his wife, going out all weathers, standing about, cracking the occasional head. There was more to life. He and his wife, Maureen, sold up and moved to the coast, where they opened a small newsagent's. Their new-found life style seemed far more in keeping with their new found requirements: it was a far more pedestrian lifestyle for one thing, and they both flourished because of it.

Michael, as promised, gave away all his merchandise to anyone who wanted it, and there were many that did. It didn't seem to bother them that none of it was genuine, not as long as it was free gratis and for nothing. Having dispensed with everything he had in his case, he then chose to return to the warehouse in Bermondsey and replenish his stock. By doing that, he naturally, had to explain to his former colleagues what his intentions were. It went without saying that once they learnt of his plans, they weren't particularly happy about it. An argument had ensued. Michael, as might be expected, came off the worst for it. On the back of this he chose to move further away and start over again....and it had to be said, having decided to do that, he prospered because of it.

Beyond Redemption

Being the 23rd December

Standing in a shop doorway, of a site no longer occupied, the Devil watched the occasional flurry of snow as it gently fell into the street. Upon his arrival, the doorway had been already taken up by a homeless individual, who was using it as a permanent residence. As he was expecting to meet a colleague there very soon, and not wanting to share the doorway with anyone, he offered the man a thousand pounds to make himself absent for a time. After having gotten over the initial shock of being offered such a munificent sum, to do something that was only too familiar to his habits anyway, he was only too willing to take himself off for the required spell; and was now in search of other erstwhile thermal provision. And, so the Devil waited patiently, knowing that it was a required condition, as his collaborator as he liked to think of his colleague was always invariably tardy in his habits.

Consulting his pocket watch, for the second time, in as many minutes, and having muttered the words 'Incessantly late' beneath his breath, a voice from behind him suddenly announced.

"Yo, Scratch, my main man! How's things and how's it hanging?"

The voice offered an unmistakable offensive timbre about it, as if it knew who he was and didn't give a hoot about it, come what may.

Looking up, the Devil saw a tall, lean, gaunt individual standing before him. The figure stood nearly seven feet in height, and looked altogether pail in complexion and terribly wan in appearance, as if a dozen or so hearty meals might have done him the world of good. He wore a long ragged black cape, that looked most shabby and mottled and was visibly torn to a high degree at the base. This in itself would have marked the person out as being a trifle odd, or slightly eccentric at the very least, but in addition to this he also carried a long wicked looking two-handed scythe, that was slung casually across his left shoulder - which seemed to infer that if nothing else, he at least meant business, business that might not be of an altogether compassionate nature.

"You're late!" snapped the Devil, irritably.

The man held his hands wide by way of an explanation.

"Places to go, my man – people to see, etc. etc. No rest for the wicked as they say. Anyway, I say how's it hanging, Scratchy?" he asked.

The Devil bit his lip and held his temper. This meeting was going to be fraught with significant frustration and exasperation, he could tell from the outset.

"May I ask, is that farm implement really necessary on this occasion?" he asked, ignoring the innuendo and indicating the scythe. "Don't you think it might possibly be regarded as a little too panto-ish, I mean especially for the time of year that is?"

The figure looked lovingly at the scythe, and stroking it, shook his head.

"What, this? Nah! Goes with the job. Stock in trade and all that. And as Death, I wouldn't be seen without it, now, would I? It'd be a bit like a carpenter without a hammer, or a car mechanic without a spanner, wouldn't it? And people expect it of me. And anyway, what's all the fuss about, I mean no-one can see me only you, unless I choose otherwise. So, what's the big deal anyway? You rarely bother me unless it's something on an epic scale. So, what are we talking about here, Scratch, plague, genocide, an extinction event? Whatever it is, I'm sure it's going to be great fun and I'm up for it. Man, do you remember the year fourteen twenty-nine? Boy was that memorable! Plague sweeping across Europe like there was no tomorrow, people dropping like flies by the thousand, there were. What a bash that was. A real humdinger and no mistake. Well, what's it to be, Scratchy?"

The Devil closed his eyes, bit his lip for the second time, and briefly held his breath. There were few things he found totally insufferable, but being referred to as 'Scratch' or 'Scratchy' in such an intimate and familiar tone, and being asked 'how it was hanging', was two of them. Death, unfortunately, had this irritating habit of showing very little respect to anyone, but it was something the Devil had learned to live with over time; and it had to be said that, despite his short-comings, Death did occasionally have his uses, so it sometimes paid to just grin and bear it, if at all possible.

"There's a rather unsavoury character we are about to visit," said the Devil. "And I would very much appreciate it, once we do, if you might perform your party piece, that is, when prompted to do so. You see, in short, I wish to scare the hell out of him, should it come to that."

Death frowned and scratched his head a little.

"Well, I suppose I can do, that is if you absolutely insist," he said. "But is that it? I mean, isn't that more your line than mine? It's definitely more your area of expertise. You're forgetting, I've seen you in full flow, remember? And I have to say, in all fairness, you're pretty good at it, too. Always scares the bejeezus out of me, every time. Oops. Bear with me just a minute. Duty calls and all that. Won't be a tick."

As the Devil watched him, and with a sense of growing irritation and unease, Death snook up behind an elderly couple, who were linked arm in arm, and gently touched the man on the shoulder. In an instant the man, groaned loudly and fell to the floor. This caused quite a stir, and immediately a small group of people began gathering themselves about him on the pavement in order to administer help if required. Someone took out a phone and rang for an ambulance, whilst another felt for his pulse and announced that they couldn't find one and that the gentleman appeared to have died.

"Was that really quite necessary?" the Devil asked, disapprovingly. "A trifle distasteful, don't you think? And just before Christmas, as well. Absolutely shocking behaviour. You should be thoroughly ashamed of yourself."

Death looked altogether surprised by the question and once again spread his palms in a gesture of surprise.

"Distasteful? No, not at all. What was distasteful about it? His time was up. That was that. You have to be pragmatic in this line of work. I don't make the rules, or have you forgotten?" And he pointed upwards to the sky with the scythe, with a certain poignancy. Shrugging resignedly, the Devil chose to move on and not labour the point.

As they slowly began to make their way up the Charing Cross Road, the Devil began to detect a certain lassitude in Death's mood and wondered if his silence could be attributed to him wanting to be elsewhere. Perhaps the prospect of performing his party-piece once again failed to ignite the passions that usually held sway when the thought of morbidity, or anything approaching it, was on the horizon. This being so, he enquired of him.

"Is everything all right with you? Only you appear a little maudlin, if you don't mind my pointing out."

Death stopped mid-stride.

"Yeah, I'm fine," he replied, coolly. "It's just that there's something that has been playing on my mind now. Has done for some time. I was just wondering if you had ever considered death, that's all."

This question caused the Devil to frown somewhat, as he regarded it an unusual and unnecessary issue. Why would the Grim Reaper ask him if he had ever considered Death? He tried not to think of him at all, in fact ever, if truth be known.

"Well, I suppose if I was honest I very rarely give you a second thought, unless of course I require your services. And I don't wish to sound insensitive, but as you can imagine I'm a great advocate of 'telling the truth and shaming the Devil'. There's no offence meant, of course."

"That's not what I meant at all," said Death, shaking his head. "I mean, have you ever considered the sheer act of dying, and if so, what it would mean for you. I have, and to be honest I think of very little else nowadays. It seems to haunt my thoughts a lot. Far too much to be truthful."

The question was a puzzler, and no mistake, and caused the Devil to reflect upon it intently for a moment or two. Death apparently spent most of his time considering death, and that was to be expected, surely? It was his job, after all. But the actual thought of Death going through the process of dying, that just didn't bear thinking about. It was unnatural for one thing and went against the very order of things.

"Well, in all honesty, I have to say I have never given any serious consideration to the matter," he replied. "I'm immortal for one thing, and so are you, so why would it concern us?"

Death became rather pensive and began to shuffle his feet nervously.

"Just a thought," he said.   "What you must try and understand is that I see death in all its infinite glory, every day of the week – people and things shuffling off this mortal coil, and what not. And it's great, love it, don't get me wrong, I absolutely adore my job; live for it. There's nothing more satisfying than watching either an individual keel over, or a crowd getting blitzed by a lightning bolt, or atomized by a meteorite. But I can't help thinking that somewhere along the line I'm missing out, you know? As though dying just might be a nice thing to do."

The Devil looked horrified at the very notion of it.

"A nice thing to do? What in the name of salvation has gotten into you? And what I ask would be nice about it?" he asked. "The very notion is totally irrational and not to say in the least – absurd!"

Death continued to shuffle his feet, looking and sounding most unsure of himself.

"I think what I'm trying to say is, I believe it might provide a bit of a break from the norm, that's all – and we could all do with one of those from time to time, don't you think? A break, I mean. I know I could."

"But you can't have Death, dying." The Devil pointed out.

"Oh, oh, and why ever not? It seems a pretty natural thing to do to me. And no-one knows more about it than I do, believe me. And let's have a bit of fairness and impartiality about it, that's all I'm asking. You're not being deathist, are you by any chance? And what difference would it make you, anyway, if I pegged it? None at all as far as I can see. And it wouldn't need to be permanent. Just like a bit of a sabbatical."

The Devil found himself near speechless with the concept of it all and shook his head in bewilderment.

"Well, it's a contradiction in terms, for one thing. And what's more it is totally illogical and completely absurd. It's a loony idea."

Death pulled a long expression.

"I fail to see why," he said, sounding a trifle peevish. "If it's good enough for every other living thing then it's good enough for me. Makes perfect sense."

"Well, if you honestly believe that, then may I suggest that you give the matter some serious thought," replied the Devil. "You seem to be forgetting that you are the apotheosis of mortality; you personify the end of all things as we know them. Any living creature clutching on to the vestiges of life will attest to that. Remove death from the equation and you remove the very cycle of life, the very cornerstone of existence itself. And if that were to happen then nothing would ever pass away now, would it? Everything existing would continue to proliferate, until the whole of the world was over run with the un-dead. Chaos would inevitably ensue. The whole idea is gross and goes against the very order of things."

"That's as may be," said Death, defensively. "But all I'm saying is I think it would be a nice break from the norm, that's all…. Perhaps I could just resign – you know, hand in my notice. Never thought of that before. Needs some consideration, does that."

The Devil watched in disbelief as Death continued on with his journey up the Charing Cross Road, scythe swung casually over one shoulder. Then after he had gone a few yards, he made a great effort to call out after him.

"Believe me, it wouldn't work – I know, I've tried it!"

Soho:

During its early years, this had been an area of London that was full of both vice and corruption, and in equal measure. The local authority was only too willing to turn a blind eye to what was going on there, as long, that is, their palms were well and truly greased, and on a regular basis. It was only in time, and with a more enlightened approach, that the corrupt individuals had finally been weeded out; but even so, vice here still played its part, only it was more difficult to spot.

-0-

The two finally arrived at what appeared to be a fairly inconspicuous looking glass door to a building in Pinner Street. It lay firmly between two Chinese restaurants and looked most unobtrusive and totally unremarkable. It did, in fact, seem so unassuming that it was without a doubt something you would never look at twice and would pass by without a second thought. And this was precisely what it was intended to impress upon people. It consisted of a large piece of frosted glass, that not only obscured vision, but also made it impossible to determine what exactly was taking place on the other side of it.

"Is this it?" asked Death, sounding altogether disappointed by what he was seeing, whilst tapping the glass with the point of his scythe.

"Yes, this is our port of call." returned the Devil.

"It's a bit nondescript, don't you think?"

The Devil very slowly and thoughtfully ran his gloved hand over the glass.

"Yes, I suppose it is," he admitted, "Very nondescript. But you may take it from me that it covers a multitude of sins, nonetheless."

Death, shrugged, braced himself and immediately began to inflate. His skin fell away to reveal bleached white bones and a skull that radiated malevolence and a great deal of malice and ill-will.

"What do you think you are doing?" asked the Devil, endeavouring to maintain a modicum of patience, and finding it very hard going.

Death stopped his transformation and reverted back to his true form.

"I thought you wanted me to do my party-piece?" he said, sounding a tad perplexed and not to say a little disappointed. "I was just about to go in and frighten everyone to death. Isn't that what you wanted?"

The Devil took a deep breath, doing his level best to maintain his composure.

"No, that isn't why I asked you here," he said, garnering as much self-possession as possible. "I merely wish you to observe; and then, should I give you the go ahead –

you may then do what you do best. Have I made myself clear on this point?"

Death nodded, though it had to be said, he did look somewhat disillusioned by it all and altogether thwarted in his desired intentions.

"Very well, what's it to be then, my man?" he asked.

"Just follow quietly behind me, until I say otherwise," said the Devil, patiently. "And kindly remain obscured to all and sundry."

"Okay. You're the boss. Who exactly is in there by the way?"

"Someone who is, shall we say, comparable to a very large boil on the backside of humanity," returned the Devil, and then added with great emphasis.

"And he is a boil I am about to lance, once and for all."

And, so saying he pressed the door bell and waited. After a moment the door opened ever so slightly, so slightly in fact that no-one could be seen on the other side of it. A voice growled: 'Who is it, and what do you want?'

"It's Nicholas to see, Mr. James Pearson," the Devil replied, in what could only be interpreted as the politest of tones.

"Nicholas? Nicholas who?" asked the voice.

"Oh, just, Nicholas," said the Devil.

"Your name ain't on my list, so sod off," came the curt voice, and the door quickly closed on them.

"I could kill him, if that would help," said Death, eager to make himself useful. "It would take less than an instant for me to go in and kill all of them, then we could be on our way."

The Devil shook his head in an ongoing gesture of tolerance.

"That really won't be necessary. Our purpose here is to see one man, and that man is James Pearson. His cohorts are of little interest to me, well at least for now. Maybe at a later date, perhaps. But this particular gentleman is of great interest to me; though, my purpose here is purely salutary, I can assure you. He has become a millstone that has become attached to a very large albatross, which has in turn become inexorably entwined around the neck of society. And I am here, merely, to shall we say rectify matters."

"So, what do we do now?" asked Death. "I assume you aren't going to give this guy the benefit of the doubt, then, not like you sometimes do?"

"Oh, I always do that," replied the Devil. "Though it has to be said, I doubt very much he will accept the offer. Knowing him as I do. I may, of course, be wrong in that assumption. Time, as they say, will inevitably tell."

Without further ado, the Devil pushed the door, which opened upon his touch, and went in. Death closely followed on behind.

As they entered, the voice they had encountered earlier showed itself to have a body; it was a real brute, feral and definitely of low intelligence. Turning, it surveyed the Devil, and spoke.

"I thought I just locked that door!" it growled.

"Well, did you now?" said the Devil.

"Yes, I damn well did – and you're leaving! Get your arse out of here, before I'm obliged to throw you out!"

"Let me kill him," said Death, eagerly raising his scythe.

The Devil waived him aside rather irritably. Death could be so wearing at times.

"No – no – no! Death is not necessary! It isn't always the solution to every problem you happen to encounter. I do wish that you would take that on board!"

"It's Death you're talking to here," replied Death solemnly. "It's what I do, remember?"

The brute stopped in his tracks, now thinking he was dealing with a lunatic, who was talking to himself.

"Who are you talking to?" he asked, not being party to Death's presence.

"No-one of importance," replied the Devil.

"Oh, thanks for the vote of confidence," said Death.

The brute raised an arm that was altogether reminiscent of a short telegraph pole, and made to eject the Devil forcibly with it. Upon laying his hand upon the Devil's person, however, his whole demeanour suddenly changed; straight away he looked confused and his speech became disordered and muddled.

"I – er…I…um…I'm not sure what I was doing…What was I doing?" he asked, placing a hand to his forehead, his thoughts now in total disarray.

Smiling, the Devil took his arm and led him towards the door.

"I believe you were just in the process of going for a bite to eat, Charlie. And what a great idea that is, I have to say. You must be ravenous, what with all that standing around all morning, throwing out would be interlopers into the street. Must give you a bit of appetite I would have thought."

"…Was I?" Charlie, looking most uncertain, rubbed his chin and asked. "Is that what I was going to do? I mean, are you sure about that?"

The Devil nodded in affirmation.

"Why, most assuredly," he said. "I can guarantee it. You take yourself off and have a good time. I will hold the fort here while you are gone. Be an absolute pleasure."

"Er - Th – Thank you – Well, if you're sure then."

"Absolutely. You have a sticky bun or a mince pie while you're at it. You deserve it. Go and enjoy yourself."

Charlie's face took on an even more confused and vacant look, as if he desperately was trying to remember something of great importance, but couldn't.

"I'm sure there was something I had to do," he said, looking most bewildered. "Now, what was it?"

"Nothing of importance," assured the Devil. "You run along, have a good time and take the rest of the day off. I will cover for you."

Charlie, now seemingly reassured by the Devil's words, left them to continue their journey downwards into the bowels of the building, and whatever awaited them below. As they went, the Devil heard Death mutter under his breath: 'Immolation would have been quicker'.

A single unattractive door blocked their entrance. Not feeling that the general courtesy of knocking was required in this instance, the Devil turned the handle and walked straight in.

"Christmas felicitations!" he called brightly, to a short fat man sitting behind a desk. Visibly taken aback by the Devil's sudden and unexpected entrance, the man stood up, revealing that he was only marginally taller than when he was sitting.

"Who the bleedin' 'ell are you!" he shouted. "And where's Charlie gone? He's supposed to be manning the door! The useless pile of puss! Where is he gone?"

The man made his way to the door and looked up the stairs, only to have his convictions confirmed: Charlie was indeed nowhere to be seen.

"He's gone for a quick bite to eat," explained the Devil. "Oh, and a coffee, I believe. Said he needed a break."

"A break! A coffee?!" raged the man. "He's gone for a bloody coffee! I'll roast his nuts over a hot fire for this!"

The Devil chose this moment to take a seat. Taking off his gloves, he waited patiently for the short man to recover himself. Death stood close behind endeavouring to look useful.

"Why don't you make yourself at home?" bawled the short man, returning to the other side of the desk.

"Why, that's most kind," returned the Devil. "Like the décor, by the way. Perhaps a little too much kitsch for my tastes, but liveable. Now, if I may make a suggestion, I strongly advise that you sit yourself down, before you have a coronary. You look as though you are about to implode. It can't be healthy for you, it really can't."

And the Devil was correct in this assumption, the man did, for all the world look as though he was about to both implode and explode at the same time.

"GET YOUR ARSE OUT OF THAT CHAIR - AND GET OUT OF MY OFFICE!!!" he screamed, his face turning a most unhealthy shade of purple and plum colours, that continually appeared to merge and coalesce. Seeming not to take any notice of the man's demand, the Devil continued to sit quietly, taking in the décor. All the while, Death stood in one corner, still unseen, and amused himself by flicking through a glamour calendar on the wall.

"Have you ever read Sun Tzu's - The Art of War?" asked the Devil, poignantly.

"THE WHAT?!!!" howled the small man, now very near to being apoplectic with rage.

"The Art of War, by Sun Tzu? It's a captivating read," continued the Devil, sounding as unflappable as it is possible to get. "It precisely sets out the best and most decisive way to deal with an enemy, or an opponent for that matter. You could learn a lot from it. I really would heartily recommend it. Oh, James, please do sit down. You have a large vein in the side of your neck that is currently pulsating at such a pronounced rate, I seriously believe, if not quelled, and soon, it is likely to burst. Now, do take a seat old man, there's a good chap, before you drop dead with a cerebral haemorrhage."

The small man approached the Devil, his hands clasping and unclasping in violent spasms of rage. No-one had ever spoken to him like this before. No-one had ever dared.

"How the 'ell do you know my name?" he demanded to know.

"It goes with the territory," said the Devil, calmly.

Events had apparently now gone too far for the little man. Lurching towards his desk, he hastily pushed a button on an intercom and bawled into the device.

"BENNY – LENNY! Get your arses in here and be quick about it!"

Within a matter of seconds, a door to the rear of the office opened and in rushed two very large men. Both of them could easily have been related to Charlie, such was their size and demeanour.

"What is it, Mr Pearson?" asked one of them.

"I want you to throw this prat into the street – and do it NOW!" said the little man, and then quickly added. "No, wait. Take him round the back in the alley, first, and make him wish he had never stepped foot in this office. And then go out and find that lumbering imbecile, Charlie and bring him back here so I can kick his nuts – and be quick about it!"

"Yes, Mr Pearson," said the second man, and without the need for any further prompting from James, they approached the Devil in a very menacing manner, and with every intention of fulfilling their boss's wishes. But before either man could lay a hand upon him, the Devil lifted a finger and brought them both to a shuddering halt.

"Gentlemen!" he said, calmly and without undue haste. "Your colleague, Charlie, has taken himself off for a coffee and an early lunch. Now, why don't you both do the same? If you're fortunate you just might catch up with him. But don't dawdle, will you?"

As had been witnessed earlier, with Charlie, a look of complete resignation came over the men's faces.

"Er, yeah, yeah that sounds like a plan," avouched the second man. "What do think, Lenny?"

Lenny looked thoughtful.

"Yeah, sounds good, Benny, sounds good," he said. "Suits me. Shall we be off then?"

They both turned to leave and headed towards the door. A scream, however, rang out that brought them both up short.

"WHERE THE HELL DO YOU TWO NUMBSKULLS THINK YOU ARE GOING?" howled the little man.

Both men looked somewhat confused by the question, unsure of what the problem was. It was Lenny who answered.

"Your friend said that we could cut out for a bit of lunch, Mr Pearson."

"LUNCH! LUNCH! You pair of idiotic, retarded pricks! I'm the one who pays your wages! Take this bastard outside; take him somewhere quiet, and kick seven bells out of him! Have you both got that?"

"Yes, sir, Mr Pearson," said Benny. "Straight away, sir."

The two men, then without a second thought, left the office, leaving the short man standing with his mouth agape, hardly able to comprehend what he was seeing.

"Do sit down, James. You are taking on the look of a large guppy that has just found itself out of water," said the Devil. "Not a pretty sight, believe me. It's fair turning my stomach."

The small man, however did nothing of the sort. Instead, he stood pointing an accusatory finger at his unwelcome visitor.

"You've paid 'em off! You lousy bastard! You've paid 'em all off, haven't you! Who was it? Who's put you up to this? Was it Danny Madden? No, I know who it was – it was that bastard, Chalky Pitch, wasn't it? Yes, I bet it was that son of a bitch! I'll have his nuts for this, so help me I will! Look, I don't know who you are, but whatever it is they are paying you I will double it – no, I will treble it! You can retire and go anywhere in the world. I'll look after you, and that's a promise. You fall in with me. Do we have a deal? Yes?"

For a brief moment the Devil looked as though he was seriously considering the offer; staring at his hands and shaking his head, as if weighing up all the pros and cons of it all. Then, apparently having made his mind up, he looked the little man squarely in the eye with an intensity that made the other squirm.

"James Pearson, aka Jimmy the Pill. An altogether bizarre, though rather apt, nom de guerre, I think. Jimmy-the-Pill, the largest supplier of designer drugs in the whole of the Capital; one of the greatest purveyors of misery and despair that has ever walked the hallowed streets of this wonderful city. So, Jimmy – what you must now ask yourself is, why am I here? What is my true purpose, whilst sitting in this seat in your office? Is it to mayhap, to bring you to your senses, and may be to ask you to turn over a new leaf – perhaps help you to see the light, as it were? Or, is the answer a little more prosaic? Maybe I'm here merely to put a bullet in you? Now, that would rectify matters, wouldn't it? A bullet? What do you think?"

The little man turned ashen and sank further down into his seat, believing that his end was nigh. It was not a pleasant sight to behold.

"I'll pay you whatever you ask," he said, pleading. "Just name your figure, anything, anything at all."

Ignoring his entreaties, the Devil continued.

"My purpose in being here, James, is purely constructive, nothing more. You have become a rather unwieldly millstone around society's neck. It has become like a fetid, rancid noose, choking the very life out of it, and it is all of your creation. And I am here purely to rectify matters. I am here to put things right; to redress the balance, if you like. But before I do that, you are going to accompany me. We are going on a little journey together – you may call it a journey of discovery if you so wish. But one I feel you will surely benefit from."

As the Devil finished speaking, James made a grab for a drawer in his desk. Hastily rummaging through it in an attempt to locate something.

"I'm going nowhere with you, chummy, as you are about to discover to your cost!" he shrieked loudly.

Watching his exploits with a conditioned eye, the Devil merely waited patiently for him to finish. Having finally found what he was looking for, James pulled out a very large and unwieldy looking gun and brandished it in the Devil's direction, his confidence now seemed fully restored, he remained belligerent and seemingly in full control of the situation. Needless to say, he wasn't.

"Right, now it's time for some answers!" he growled. "Who was it who sent you here – and I want none of your bullshit – I want straight answers, do you understand!"

"Oh, I see," said the Devil. "Straight answers, is it?" he asked, resignedly.

"Yes, straight answers – and if they are not to my liking, you will be leaving here in a bloody box pal! Do I make myself understood?"

The Devil pursed his lips thoughtfully, before answering.

"Yes, you do indeed, James, you most certainly do. A box. So, you want the whole truth? And by that, I mean everything? Nothing is to be held back? Is that correct? Warts and all?"

"Too damn right, nothing's to be held back - and hurry up about it!"

The Devil rose from his seat and replaced his gloves, all the while, Death looked on with growing interest.

"Very well – if that's how it's to be - the whole truth you want and the whole truth you shall have. In answer to who it was that sent me here, the simple answer is, it was me, I did. Though the names Danny Madden and Chalky Pitch are known to me, I can state quite categorically, hand on heart, that I have never met either of these gentlemen before. Though you may rest assured that they are both on my 'To do' list in the near future."

"I get it!" James snarled, waving the gun beneath the Devil's nose. "So, you think you can just waltz in here as free as you like, pay off my boys, and take over my operation? Well, let me tell you my friend, it ain't gonna happen! Did you really think it would be so easy? Do you seriously think you're the first one to try and pull this stunt? Let me tell you, there's a number of flyovers around here that can attest to those that thought they could – and they all failed! Every last one of 'em. Take over my bleedin' operation?! The devil you will!"

The Devil nodded.

"Yes, right on both accounts," he said. "And now, if you have finished with your empty threats and overzealous paranoia, we can get on, only the day moves along at an alarming rate and I still have very much to do."

"You, arrogant piece of shit!" screamed James. Raising his gun, he aimed at the Devil and fired – once – twice – three times – and then a fourth, just for good measure. The Devil clutched his chest, staggered back and then surprised his assailant by smiling broadly.

"Well, now you've had your fun and games, I suggest that we really do make a move. So much to do and so little time. It's always the true enemy, you know. Oh, and please close your mouth. It's becoming a rather bad habit of yours. And do stop waving that gun about. Yes, the bullets are real – and no, no-one has swapped them for blanks while your back was turned. Let's just say I'm slightly immune to them. Good, now that's established, let's please make a move."

Upon saying this, the room began to take on a darker and much more grave appearance. Gone was the desk, the chairs and the pictures that had adorned the walls only seconds earlier – all to be replaced, by a building that boasted neither windows nor doors. The place they now found themselves in was severely austere, with water dripping in torrents down the walls. Every part of the structure was a living tribute to the very worst sort of degradation known to man. Rubbish and filth lay everywhere, stacked up in undisturbed heaps, allowing only the rats to ply their trade with anything approaching satisfaction. The Devil casually moved through the building like an old pro, with James, who was now in a severe state of shock, following meekly behind, gun hanging limply from his hand like a broken appendage. Entering one particular room, though to be more precise it was more akin to a pit than a room, their noses were assailed by the worst kind of stench imaginable. It was an admixture of stale vomit and ordure, mixed with stagnant urine. It caused James to recoil visibly and reel from the room, making all further transition impossible for him.

"Dear God!" he screamed, doing his utmost to cover his nose and mouth to drive out the stench. "What's causing this stink?"

Unfazed by it all, the Devil casually replied.

"Why, it's human waste, James, that is, in the main. Come closer, come and witness at first hand the end result of all your insignificant labours upon this earth. I feel it will both shock and surprise you."

"Mine?" asked James, horror struck. "What do you mean, mine? What have I to do with any of this?"

"Why, you appear surprised. Don't you supply the drugs that these people ingest, drugs that because of their all-consuming addiction, have reduced them all to this pitiable and pathetic state? This is the end result, James – Look upon your earthly works of devastation and witness what you have created here. Tell me, does it make you proud, are you pleased by what you see?"

James forced himself to move slightly further into the room, but beyond that he could not go, try as he might. As he looked about, he could just make out in the shadows numerous people within; most of them were lying on sodden mattresses. Every one of them was wretched, malnourished, worthless and despicable. In this establishment food always took a back seat, with the ever-present need for drugs taking precedent. Backing out of the room again in total disgust and horror, James blurted out as he did so:

"This ain't my doing! No way! I'm not responsible for any of this, pal! No, sir! You've got that all wrong!"

"Oh, but you are, James," corrected the Devil. "You are wholly responsible. You are the sole perpetrator here, and no-one else. You, James Pearson – Jimmy the Pill. Gaze upon your works and despair, if true man you be. Has your heart become so petrified that you cannot feel anything for these poor wretches, these lost and wayward souls? Are you so beyond redemption, that even now, when you teeter upon the very precipice of eternal damnation, you cannot admit to your wicked ways?"

James backed further out of the room, holding up his hands in defence as he did so, using them as a stalwart against impending blame.

"You're not laying the blame for this at my door!" he bawled and backed away even further. "I'm not taking the rap for this shit. These people ain't even real! You just made em up! It's a dream, an illusion, that's what it is! And, anyway, if they were real, they're just filth, that's what they are! They're human dross; scum, pieces of shit, every last one of 'em. They don't warrant anything half decent! And they don't get any sympathy from me. Nobody forces 'em to take it, it's all their own doing, not mine! They deserve everything that's coming to them!"

The Devil stood watching him, his eyes narrowing by the second and along with them any further possibility of James' redemption.

"You refuse to take any blame for what you have witnessed here?" he asked, his voice now beginning to simmer with fierce intent that even now went unnoticed, except by Death, who continued to stand quietly by, observing.

"Too bloody right I do! You can take all this and poke it as far as I'm concerned."

"Then, so be it," said the Devil. "We shall now return from whence we came. Your future is set by your own denial! You have made your decision and you may now live with it."

In a trice the two of them were back in the office, with not so much as a paper-clip out of place. The Devil carefully pulled his collar up around his neck, turned to leave, and then turned back for the last time.

"James, before I leave you, I would like to know if you are familiar with The Book of Revelation?"

"The what?" asked James, feeling that another bad experience was imminent, but even so felt that he was up to it.

The Devil continued.

"The Book of Revelation – book six to be more precise. The Four Horsemen of the Apocalypse. Let me quote you a brief summation. For I feel it rather apt here. 'And there entered the pale rider, and upon his brow was written Death – and all hell followed.' You may do well to consider that at length. A sobering thought. Now, before I take my final leave of you, I would like to tell you a little something about myself. I sincerely believe that you will find it altogether enlightening. Throughout my entire existence, I have always been present here on earth, in various guises, of course. And during all that time, I have seen eons come and go, I have seen long standing empires crumble into dust, and I have looked on casually as entire dynasties were wiped from the very face of the earth, never to be seen again; I have witnessed mighty King's humbled, prostrating themselves before me, begging for forgiveness for all their earthly transgressions; and, during all that time, I have walked the earth with an open mind, judging only as and when I deemed it necessary. And I do so now, once again. And yet I get no gratification from it, James. None at all.

There, I have finished. And now I would like to introduce you to a colleague of mine. I feel sure that the pair of you will get along splendidly, as you are both very much involved in the same line of work. I really believe that you should hit it off swimmingly." And then, just as he turned to go, Death finally made an appearance, allowing himself to be seen for the first time. James, upon seeing him, looked horrified and retreated further into the room.

"Who the hell is this?" he asked, looking on in total panic and ever-growing alarm. The Devil didn't respond. Instead, he made slowly for the exit, quietly closing the door as he left. Then, as he rested his foot upon the first step of the stair-case, leading to the street, soul wrenching screams could be heard issuing forth from the office behind him. By the time he had reached the street above, they had stopped altogether, leaving behind a silence that was nothing short of tangible.

After word

James' mind was a whirl – a veritable whirl of vivid memories and nightmarish visions. It had all been so clear, so seemingly real. But was it? Everything was so confused, his thoughts so disordered. Where was he? Come to think of it, who was he? Nothing appeared to make any sense anymore. He was aware of a biting cold, so very cold. It seeped through his clothes and infiltrated the very marrow of his bones. His head hurt intolerably and he had this overwhelming feeling of lethargy, brought on by he knew not what. And the murk and gloom, it was everywhere, intense and overwhelming. He became aware of others around him. Their plight appeared similar to his own. They were thin rakish figures, pathetic and self-absorbed. Then, he was aware of an odour. It was a terrible odour. An almost unworldly stench. Where had he encountered that before? Somewhere. Memories were so obscure, so ambiguous. Then, deep within the recesses of his mind something stirred. He felt sure it must be important – but it was so obtruse, perplexing, so distant. But what did it matter? It didn't. Why should it? Only one thing mattered…. It mattered more than life itself…. the drugs…yes, the drugs…there was nothing else.

The Final Assignment

Being Christmas Eve

Leicester Square was positively alive with a thronging mass of people, when the Devil arrived. His morning, had been inundated with him dispensing good cheer and festive spirit to all and everyone he met. And it had to be said, he was now feeling the after affects of all his efforts, not physical you understand, as he didn't ever get tired, but it was more an overwhelming feeling of joy and wonder at the magic of Christmas. Looking around for a bench upon which he could sit for a few minutes, purely to get to grips with it all, it soon became apparent to him that all those available were already fully occupied. Never mind. It was a problem, definitely, but not an insurmountable one. With no more than a thought, a comfortable bench became available to him. He sat down upon it with much satisfaction, stretched out his legs, closed his eyes and began to soak up the Christmas ambience that he enjoyed so much. As he sat there relaxing, a feeling of overwhelming oneness slowly began to spread itself through his tired frame, draping him like a warm blanket. Ah, the sheer joy of Christmas – there was nothing quite like it, he thought. After a brief moment or so, he became aware of someone else sitting upon his bench. This surprised him mightily, as it should not have been possible; when he thought it into existence, he purposefully included a proviso that no-one else could use it but himself; a trifle selfish, admittedly, but then, he never professed to being perfect, hence his job title. As he looked along the bench to observe the trespasser, he saw that it turned out to be an elderly, portly gentleman, with long white hair and an equally long white beard and a somewhat florid expression – and what is more to the point, he was looking straight at him, and smiling broadly. As the Devil continued to gaze at the man, the other suddenly spoke:

"Hello, Nick!" he said, sounding a most amiable and jolly kind of fellow.

"Hello, Nick," returned the Devil, with equal equanimity. "How are things panning out for you this year? Busy, I would imagine."

"Oh, much of a muchness," replied the portly gentleman. "The naughty list seems to grow ever longer year after year. Most disappointing I have to say. Anyhow, I'm just taking a little time out before the onset later. Thought I would stop by and see how things were progressing. Going to be busy this year, as you rightly point out. A lot to do. And you?"

"Bit of this – bit of that," replied the Devil, nonchalantly. "Nothing really to write home about. You know how it is. Different faces, same old challenges. Things rarely change."

"And all this is culminating when, exactly?" asked the gentleman.

"Tonight, actually. Not unlike yourself."

As they chatted, the Devil noticed out of the corner of his eye, that two young children, a girl aged about eight and a boy of about six, were standing staring at his associate most intently. The girl then made a move, having gathered up her confidence and was the first to speak. Shuffling forward in a shy, coy fashion, she then whispered to the portly gentleman:

"My brother says that you are the real Father Christmas, because you are fat and you have a white beard like he does, but I don't believe it. I said to him that the real Father Christmas would be at the North Pole and not here in Leicester Square."

The portly gentleman looked up, exchanged glances with the Devil, smiled, and then replied:

"Well, your brother is most astute, I think young lady. He's very clever, indeed. And what is more, he is correct, I am none other than Father Christmas, or Santa Claus, though my name is really, Nicholas. Coincidentally, the very same as my friend here."

The young girl casually looked at the Devil, but with little interest, before turning her attention back to Santa Claus.

"Is he an elf?" she asked.

"Well, er, no, no not really. I think we can safely say that he doesn't fall into the category of 'one of Santa's little helpers, though he does have a purpose all of his own. Which is probably best not to dwell on."

"But are you the REAL Father Christmas?" she persisted. "I mean the real real one, and not somebody just dressed up, like one of those fat old men in the stores?"

"Yes, I am none other," he asserted. "I am really Father Christmas. The one and only."

The girl's eyes widened, noticeably. And all she could say was:

"Wow!".

Leaning forward, Santa Claus cupped his hand, and whispered in her ear.

"But you mustn't tell anyone. Do you understand? It must be our secret – yes? Can't have everyone knowing who I am, can we? That would never do."

The girl nodded in complete agreement and understanding. This caused Santa Claus to produce a red-striped candy cane out of thin air and give it to her. The girl's mouth opened even wider.

"Are you coming to our house later?" she asked.

"Indeed, I am," he replied. "Though I must insist that you are asleep when I do. And don't forget my mince pie, will you? And a carrot for the reindeer?"

The girl said that she wouldn't forget, and thanking him, turned to go. Then she quickly turned back again and asked:

"Could I have a candy cane for my brother as well, please?" she asked politely.

Santa Claus shook his head.

"No, I'm afraid not. You see, your brother, well, he's still on my naughty list, I'm afraid. Maybe when he behaves himself a little better, then we'll see."

The girl nodded in acceptance and ran off. As they watched, they saw her break her own candy cane in half and give it to the young boy, who promptly turned and stuck his tongue out at Santa Claus. They both then ran off. Turning to the Devil, Santa shrugged and pointed out.

"You see what I'm up against? Today's kids. The world is changing, Nick; changing quickly and beyond recognition, I feel." He then took out a small notebook and a pencil and began scribbling in it. "Unless he mends his ways, I'm afraid that young man will be coming your way when he gets older. And that saddens me, it really does – no offence meant, of course."

The Devil nodded in agreement.

"None taken. And I have to admit that he's on the radar, definitely on the radar," he confirmed.

"Oh dear," Santa Claus remarked. "I thought that may be the case. And, incidentally, not wishing to labour a point, but you're still on my list as well. No doubt you are aware of it?"

This time it was the Devil's turn to shrug.

"Occupational hazard, Nick. It merely goes with the job," he said, remembering the very words uttered by Death the day before.

Santa Claus pursed his lips thoughtfully.

"Yes, I suppose you have a point. Even so, I look forward to the day when I can remove it. And let us hope it is sooner rather than later, for all concerned, that is."

The Devil laughed aloud.

"And amen to that," he said. "Though if the truth be known, I believe it will remain on there for some time to come. Not that I'm advocating any conspiracy theory here, you understand. God forbid. It's just that I don't really feel that 'The Plan' calls for it yet awhile. I may be wrong. Gut reaction, you know?"

"Well, who can say?" said Santa Claus, rising from the bench. "Time no doubt will reveal all and keep us all informed. Anyhow, I really must be going now. Much to do. Tempus fugit, as they say. And they are not wrong."

"Not for you it doesn't," said the Devil blithely, only to see that Santa Claus had now disappeared altogether, leaving him alone once more.

"And that is a sign for me to be moving on, too," he said, wearily. "Still things to do. Always things to do."

Getting to his feet, he thought the bench out of existence, and as he did so he heard the sound of something hitting the floor. Looking down, he could make out a small package. It was very brightly wrapped and shimmered. Bending down to retrieve it, he turned it over. It was no larger than a matchbox and had a label attached to it. Looking at it he saw that it read: **To Nick, just a little something to keep your faith and spirits up. Yours as always, Santa Claus.** Opening it, he found it contained a small gem in the shape of a star. Holding it up to the light and examining it more closely, he noticed that it sparkled with a radiance all of its own. Smiling, he placed it into his pocket, took out his small note-book, and began flicking through its pages. Every so often, he would stop at an entry and place either a tick next to a name, or invariably cross one through. Once happy that no-one had been left out, he then turned to earlier entries, purely out of curiosities sake. As he read, he paused at a particular entry for a moment or two, simply for consideration. Then he smiled, and popped the note-book back into his pocket. Feeling altogether good about himself, and of his intentions, he moved on.

The journey to Bernier Street took him less than ten minutes to cover. He knew exactly where he was headed, and why he was going there. It had been two years since his last visit, and he had a clear vision of what to expect. When he finally arrived, he wasn't at all disappointed by what he saw. Standing outside of St Lucien's church, he surveyed the restoration work that had been carried out during his absence, and it pleased him mightily. Two years earlier the place was in imminent danger of falling down – that was until his timely intervention. Looking at the result, it satisfied him to see that it was money well spent. Apart from the underpinning of the chancel, he could see that a new notice-board now stood proudly outside, advertising the church in all its glory. In large gold lettering were painted the words Rev Adrian Noble. The Devil smiled. There was also a new set of black iron railings around its perimeter, which made the whole place seem fresh and altogether inviting. Looking back, he remembered the adversity the church had faced, and what had seemed overwhelming odds at the time. But look at it now. How those odds had been overcome in such a wonderful way. It just needed a little impetus and the will to do it; nothing more. And of course, lots of cash. That always helped.

Feeling an almost immeasurable warm sensation beginning to grow within him, he failed to notice that someone was approaching him from the rear. Then a voice caught him totally off-guard, a voice he immediately recognized and wished that he didn't.

"As I live and breathe!" it said in total astonishment. Turning, the Devil came face to face with the Reverend Adrian Noble himself. This had not been his intention at all, and it showed that he was getting sloppy and lax in his habits.

"Mr Bergdhal," continued the Reverend Noble. "Oh, this is such a delight and an answer to a prayer. I never thought for an instant that I would ever have the pleasure of seeing you again, and yet here you are. I have to admit that I'm finding it difficult to believe. And yet here you are."

The Devil smiled, reciprocating the warm greeting that he had just received.

"Why, how very good to see you again, Reverend Noble. I was just passing and couldn't resist the temptation of popping along and witnessing at first hand, how things were getting on. I must say, it all looks pretty impressive, doesn't it? Your chaps have done a marvelous job, they really have."

The Reverend Noble, near beside himself with joy at seeing his benefactor, almost shook the Devil's arm off.

"Do you know I have spent the last eighteen months endeavouring to locate you, but it has proven impossible. Your letter left no forwarding address, or anything that would have allowed me to contact you and thank you for your tremendous gift to the church. Your donation allowed us to carry out the urgent repairs required to the chancel – and far, far, more besides. It's so wonderful."

"Yes, I can see that," replied the Devil. "And as I said, the workmen have done an excellent job. You must be really pleased with it all."

He couldn't help but appreciate the irony of it all; the Devil, providing funds for the restoration of a church. If only the Reverend Noble knew the truth. It was perhaps better not to go there, he thought. No point in spoiling things and especially at Christmas, too.

"You must come along in and have a sherry and a mince pie," said the Reverend Noble, who was now in such a state of high spirits at seeing the source of his good fortune having materialised again out of the blue, he was having difficulty containing his enthusiasm. A large smile had now spread itself across his face for all the world to see. "And what is more you must provide me with an address, or a contact number at the very least, so that we can keep in touch. That is a must. I insist."

The Devil shook his head, lamentably.

"Regrettably, I'm afraid that won't be possible, Rev Noble," he said. "You see, I represent a philanthropic organisation that wish to maintain their anonymity. It is their philosophy, if you like, and they prefer to remain in the shadows. By adopting a laissez-faire attitude to what they do, it allows them to be, how shall I put it, more selective over which organisations they ultimately choose to donate to, without being in the lime-light. I'm sure you understand?"

The Reverend Noble's features fell and he looked crestfallen.

"But surely, just a small glass of sherry? As it's Christmas? I would so like to introduce you to some of my parishioners, who are currently in the church. We are holding a small carol service – and naturally to give thanks. They are all indebted to you for all of your kindness. I do know that they would love to show their appreciation. Oh, please spare us a few minutes of your time."

Turning, the Devil cursed himself for being so careless, but outwardly smiled.

"Unfortunately, as much as I would love to, my agenda doesn't allow for it," he said, feigning great disappointment. The Reverend Noble accepted the refusal with good grace. Shaking his head sadly, he said:

"Well, let us hope that one day you will be able to drop in and pay us a visit, and even stay awhile? That is, if your commitments allow you to do so."

Waving good-bye, the Devil quickly moved off, promising that one day he would do just that. Needless to say, he never did.

-0-

It was now late afternoon. Those still in gainful employment were slowly making their way home. The festive cheer and blithesome ebullience radiated across the capital; it filled every alley-way and out of the way niche to over flowing, culminating in a glorious seasonal affirmation that touched everyone it came across. The old city had never felt so good. Standing in the middle of Trafalgar Square, the Devil opened his arms wide and drank it all in. He really didn't care who saw him (and there were many that did, but they didn't care either, for the spirit that soared within them rose to seasonal heights, and they merely laughed at his antics). It was a magical time, he thought, and then he remembered what Peter Ackroyd had once said about it. *'London goes beyond any boundary or convention. It contains every wish or words ever spoken, every action or gesture ever made, every harsh or noble statement ever expressed. It is illimitable. It is infinite London'.*

And the Devil agreed wholeheartedly.

Requiem

or

What Happened After

It had begun snowing heavily again, as the Devil slowly made his way across the square to Charing Cross Station. He always used this station for his jumping off point. There was no particular reason for it, he was simply familiar with it and it made him feel comfortable. He was very much a creature of habit. As the snow began to build, he realised that by tomorrow the whole of the city would be further covered in a large white blanket of it. It would be a marvellous sight, but sadly one he wouldn't see.

Having finally finished all his tasks for that time, he chose to leave the old place to its inhabitants and their festivities. There was still plenty to be done and much to be achieved, but it would have to wait awhile. His job never, or rarely, allowed for any respite, but that was the nature of the beast. The unpredictable nature of man invariably always kept him on his toes.

Quickly crossing the street, whilst endeavouring to avoid being hit by a double-decker bus, that appeared to be running late, he made it to the station concourse in one piece. Then, without warning, a curious tingling alerted him to the fact that something there was altogether amiss. But what could it be? Looking around to see what had caused this unexpected distraction, his eye finally alighted upon the deepest recesses of the forecourt. It appeared dimly lit and from what he could see a young man was seated all alone on a bench. The place where the bench was situated was seemingly far removed and out of the way, almost as though it had been placed there specifically for natures oddities and loners. As he stood watching the young man from a distance, he became aware that he could sense nothing whatsoever about him at all. This in itself was quite remarkable, given his powers, but this young man was a completely closed book to him in every sense of the word. It seemed as if he didn't really exist. There had to be a reason for it. Curiosity piqued; he slowly made his way to where he was sitting. As he got closer, he could see that the young man lacked many things, a good bath being at the forefront of them. His hair was long, greasy and lank, and certainly didn't give the semblance of ever having encountered shampoo at any time in the recent past. Generally, the Devil was not one for passing judgement upon meeting someone for the first time, that usually came later, but even he had to admit that this kid was a complete and utter mess. The words shambolic and disorganised came to mind, amongst others.

Making his way to where the young man was sitting, he asked him:

"Do you mind if I sit here?", doing his best to sound seasonal, given the circumstances.

The young man looked up; a most miserable expression etched across his face.

"It's wet," came the curt response. "Your coat will get soaked. It's your choice."

"No, this bit's dry," said the Devil, and sure enough it was, no sooner had he thought it so. Sitting down, he caught sight of the young man's hands. As he wore no gloves, he could see that they were bright pink from the cold. Looking up, the young man could see the Devil staring at them, so hastily placed them inside the pockets of his great-coat, which looked as though it had been acquired through an army & navy store, due to its cheapness.

"You want something?" asked the young man, sounding unseasonably confrontational, whilst staring at the Devil.

"No, no, nothing whatsoever," he replied, cheerfully. "I just couldn't help but notice how unhappy you seem to be, despite the time of year, and wondered if there was anything I could do to help you. A bit of festive philanthropy, if you like."

The young man eyed him with obvious distaste and then asked in a very incisive and rude manner.

"Are you queer, or something? Because if you are then you're wasting your time and you can clear off, coz I ain't interested."

This caused the Devil to chuckle heartily at the very thought of it.

"Well, it has to be said, that in my long and chequered career, I have been accused of being many things – some of which, I must admit, have carried significant legitimacy to them – however, in direct response to your question, no, I am decidedly not – so you are perfectly safe, don't worry. And, it has to be pointed out, with no offense intended you understand, that even if I was, you do in fact carry very little appeal in that respect. In short, you stink to high heaven."

"Oh, thanks for nothing!" responded the young man.

"Don't take on. It's nothing that a good bath, and a bar of carbolic soap wouldn't put right. That's if people still use that nowadays, that is," said the Devil.

Pulling himself up-right, the young man responded to this with a certain wounded pride, as might be expected had a complete stranger told you that you stank.

"Well, maybe, you are fortunate enough to actually possess a bath! As it turns out, I don't – nor a shower for that matter; at least not any more. I imagine that you have a nice warm house, with central heating with all mod-cons – I bet you also have plenty to eat – and not forgetting, you also having loads of money in the bank, and loads of friends, who are only too willing to help you out in a pinch, should it come to it. Well, it may surprise you to learn that some of us don't have those things and I certainly don't! I have no money – no bath – no friends - nothing! Zilch! Zippo! Got it? So please don't lecture me on cleanliness! It's presently the least of my worries!"

The Devil seemed genuinely surprised by this admission.

"What? So, you have no friends at all?" he asked. "Not even one?"

"NO!" returned the young man, and gesturing to all the passers-by, continued: "Take a good look at them all, go on – each and every one of them out there is totally indifferent to what happens to me! No home – no prospects – no job, and not one of them out there gives a stuff. I am one of the faceless multitude that nobody cares about – God, how I hate every last one of them!"

"Hate is a very strong word," said the Devil. "And in my experience, like often begets like. It becomes a never-ending circle, that continually leads forever downwards. And let me assure you, that's a place you do not wish to go."

"I am past caring," replied the young man. "Anything has to be better than this! Christmas eve, homeless and without money, food or friends. It doesn't get much worse than this. And believe me when I say that you can take my word for it."

The Devil considered the young man's views.

"You have what I might regard as a somewhat querulous nature," he finally pointed out. "Not, altogether unusual in this day and age, I have to admit. But sad, nevertheless."

"I don't know what that means," returned the young man. "But if it's bad, and it contains a lot of ill-fortune, then you are probably right. I'm your man!"

The Devil was genuinely put out by the young man's deep sense of believing himself to be one of 'life's victims'. It was readily apparent that he was in a truly bad way. But even so, he saw him as a challenge, and was determined to help him out, one way or another.

"You are a definite malcontent, and it brooks no argument," he said with a chuckle. "But not beyond hope."

"I don't know what that means, either, and if it's your intention to make fun of me, then I'd sooner you didn't, as I'm not in a particularly good frame of mind, as you can probably gather. So, I'd strongly advise you to sod off, before I lose my temper."

As can be imagined, the Devil wasn't at all thrown by this outburst of seeming peevishness, and seeing that the young man was obviously beset by problems, chose a less confrontational and sanguine approach than he normally might have. Taking off one of his gloves, he held up a finger.

"Let me ask you a question," he said. "How many atoms do you think there are in this finger? And before you object to the question, or assume that I am making fun of you, I can assure you that I'm not - and there's a good reason for my asking it. So, go on, have a guess."

The young man looked bewildered, and not to say slightly irritated by the question as it didn't make much sense to him. And despite the man's assurances of not wishing to ridicule him, he wasn't altogether convinced by it.

"How many atoms in your finger? That's crazy. I've no idea. And what's the relevance, anyhow? It's a stupid question. I've been thrown out of work and my accommodation – and what's more I can't afford to pay my heating bill, or my rent, and you're asking me crazy questions like that. You're nuts."

"Please bear with me for a moment." insisted the Devil. "All will soon be revealed, I can guarantee it. You won't regret it."

Feeling it was altogether fruitless to argue the point, the young man sighed resignedly, and then said:

"I really have no idea, and to be honest with you I don't care one way or another, but let's say a hundred million, if it makes you happy. It's really no consequence to me at all. It's your finger, you deal with it."

The Devil persisted, taking no notice whatsoever of the young man's display of complete disinclination in what he had to say.

"Well, if I told you that in a grain of sand alone there are approximately two sextillions, or to be a little clearer about it, there are two thousand billion, billion, it just might give you some idea. That's quite a big number. So, you can imagine just how many there might be in a single finger. Food for thought, don't you think?"

The young man just shook his head in confusion, as he had no idea precisely what point this strange man was making.

"So?" he asked, indifferently. "It's two thousand billion, billion, in a grain of sand, so what? Who cares? Am I any better off for knowing that? Will the knowledge of it feed me over Christmas? Will it pay my rent? Or, will it help me to get another job? Well, will it?"

The Devil smiled broadly, though it had to be said, it was not a condescending smile.

"It just might," he replied.

This revelation caused the young man to sit up and pay a little closer attention to his would-be tormentor. What was the man's game? He obviously had something up his sleeve.

"So, how exactly?" he wanted to know. "How precisely is all this useless information going to improve my situation? I'm intrigued."

"Well, before I come to that, I have one more question for you, then you have my word, all will be made clear. I promise you that."

"OK, I'll buy it; fire away. I've got to hear this. What's the question? But if you're winding me up, so help me – I'll - "

The Devil smiled again, recognising that the young man was now well and truly hooked.

"Very well. My question is this: if you were to take every person in the world, that's every single one of them, mind. And you were to remove all the space there is between all the atoms that make up their respective bodies, and then squash the remainder all together, what space do you think it would it all take up? Give it some thought before you answer."

"The question's a bit weird, isn't it?" asked the young man, shaking his head.

"Indeed, it is," replied the Devil. "Indeed, it is. But very relevant, nonetheless. Just humour me here for a moment."

"All squashed together? Everything? No space left? None at all? Not one tiny bit?"

"No, none at all. Not one tiny bit."

The young man looked thoughtful.

"I'm not really sure. Let's say a house – no, a block of flats – could even be bigger. Maybe two," he said.

"No, you are wrong," said the Devil. "Would you believe it if I told you that a sugar cube is the correct answer?"

"What - never!" said the young man in total disbelief.

The Devil nodded.

"Oh, let me assure you, it's perfectly correct; a simple sugar cube – no more, no less. And the significance of all this, is? Well, I will tell you. If, as science rightly informs us, that everyone on the planet could easily be reduced to something as small as a sugar cube, meaning that each and every one; one of us consists of little more than ninety-nine per cent empty space, then I ask you this, where does that leave everyone's personalities, their hopes, their dreams, their fears, their aspirations, their frailties, their worries? Where do they all go? More to the point, knowing what you now know, where does it leave you in all this? Where are all your problems, your worries, your concerns? Etc? Etc?"

The young man's brow creased noticeably, as he appeared to consider the Devil's words most carefully. After giving the matter some considerable thought, he finally said:

"But they do exist. You can say what you like about squashing things together and all that. I know they do. They all exist…Everything does…They must exist. Every last bit of it. I'm living proof that they do. Surely, I am…Aren't I?"

"Are you? Perhaps you only think that way, because your seeming sense of reality wants you to remain that way, completely in thrall. Ask yourself, how can anything with so little solidity actually be real? The simple answer is, it can't, it's all an illusion. And it's in your mind." He then gestured to everything around him. "And I do mean, everything. Nothing is exempt. Nothing whatsoever. Everything is one big deception – and you're sitting right in the middle of it. Of course, you don't know that because the wool has been pulled firmly over your eyes."

"All an illusion?" asked the young man. "That isn't possible. It doesn't make sense to me at all."

"Oh, but it is. Everything you can sense, or more to the point, everything you think you can sense is little more than an illusion. It's little more than one big delusion, pursuing an illusion all wrapped up in a dream. What you feel, what you see, what you hear, even what you think – Everything, and there's no exception to it – none!"

"But if that is true, what purpose does it all serve? Tell me that," asked the young man. "What does any of it serve?"

"Why, veritably in sooth, my boy, it serves its very own purpose!" replied the Devil expansively. "You live in thrall. You are in a state of constant sleep; and by being so you keep the illusion alive – you feed it! The solution to all your problems is you need to wake up, and you achieve this by changing your thinking and thereby changing your very reality. It is that simple and it's the biggest thing you will ever have to deal with. Learn your lesson well – and capitalise on it."

By the look on the young man's face, it was quite obvious that he refused to accept anything that the Devil had told him.

"But it can't be that easy, if it was then everyone would be able to do it, wouldn't they? And people wouldn't continue living in poverty like they do. I mean, not having enough to eat, or to make sufficient provision for their children. Everyone would be wealthy beyond their wildest fantasies. They'd have large cars, houses and no more worries. Life would be a dream, totally idyllic, with nothing more to be concerned about."

The Devil whispered closely in his ear.

"Yes, of course, that might appear to be true, but the simple truth of the matter is very few people know about it. And if you don't know about it then you can't avail yourself of what is has to offer, can you? I heartily suggest that you try it, now, and see what happens. You have nothing to lose and a great deal to gain. You cannot gainsay it."

Looking most dubious, the young man asked.

"And how exactly am I supposed to make this miracle occur? Surely you don't expect me to just to make a wish, and then look on and see my life improve for the better? This is real life we are talking about here. And you can say what you like about all that. And at the end of the day, it's all we have. It isn't a fairy story – I'm not Aladdin and you aren't a genie either, dishing out wishes as it pleases you to do so. I believe the expression is, get real."

"True, very true!" acknowledged the Devil. "However, if you begin to visualise yourself in a more positive light, I think you might be very surprised by the results. Try it, now. Close your eyes and see yourself in better surroundings. I repeat, you have nothing to lose."

Much against his better judgement, and thinking it a complete waste of time, the young man did just that. Closing his eyes, he tried to see himself in a more positive light, all the while emphasising his feelings as being more affirmative. When he opened his eyes again, he saw that the Devil had now extended an arm in his direction. He was clutching a phone and was now offering it to him.

"What's this?" he asked, not understanding the purpose of it at all.

Smiling, the Devil replied.

"Shall we say, it's just a little festive verisimilitude, nothing more. This will connect you to your aspirations. I can guarantee it. It's an old acquaintance of mine. He and his colleagues run a charity for the homeless. They have recently come into a little good fortune, quite by chance, and are a little short staffed. Here, take it, ring him. His name is Roger. All you have to do is press CONNECT, and tell him that Nick sent you. If you do, then your life will change for the better. This is your chance to improve your existence. Don't descend further into the illusion by subjecting yourself to further negative thoughts and feelings. If you continue down that path it is difficult to find your way back. Wake up! See reality for what it really is! You have to work your way through a lot of sleep and indoctrination before you can view things as they really are. Here, take it!"

The young man gingerly reached out and accepted the phone. And as he did so the Devil rose from the bench.

"Th – thank you," he said, looking very embarrassed by the man's charitable intentions, even though he didn't comprehend what was truly taking place. "I don't know what to say."

"Say? Why, nothing is required. It's Christmas, isn't it?" replied the Devil, and winked. Then replacing his glove, he turned to go.

The young man then also rose and called out after him.

"Here, what about your phone?"

"…Keep it!" replied the Devil. "I've got plenty more."

And then in a trice he was gone.

The young man continued to watch as the Devil finally disappeared inside the station. This odd stranger, with his altogether odd philosophy on life, had granted him an opportunity to change his own life, and this could be achieved with little more than a press of his thumb.

Shortly after watching him disappear, a most unusual occurrence began to take place within the dark recess of the station forecourt. It might be imagined that the young man either made the phone call, as he had been advised to do, or even go about his business and depart on his merry way – but this is not what happened. The entire scene immediately began to change. As far as the young man himself was concerned, he now began to physically change and metamorphosise, undergoing a process of complete transmogrification: the long lank greasy hair disappeared, only to be replaced by locks of the purest samite in colour. It appeared to glow with an unusual golden inference. Youth, too, fell away, and in its turn, was replaced by a long white lustrous beard. Eyes, instantly, reflected both wisdom and an undoubted sagacious omniscience. The sombre, brooding presence that had not so long ago played such an important feature of this small corner of the station, had now also completely vanished. Not that anyone passing would have witnessed this, for what had taken place here in the last few minutes had been invisible to their eyes. And that was how it was meant to be. Gone was the bench – along with the phone, that would now never be used, and all that was left was the solitary figure unmoving in the snow, standing quietly whilst radiating a divine effulgence. A small smile played around the corners of his mouth, which was accompanied by an almost imperceptible nod, as though he were in complete agreement with something undetermined and unknown. Then, in less time than it takes to tell, he was gone, and nothing further remained to indicate whether he had ever been there at all.

-0-

After leaving the young man to a potentially better future, the Devil casually entered the station and stopped before the large clock that now showed precisely six twenty-seven. Looking up at the departures board, he could see that there was no sign for his particular destination – but then that was hardly surprising, all things considered. He paused and smiled briefly at his own conceits, and then turned and looked over his shoulder towards the route he had just taken and especially towards the section of the station where he had spoken with the young man. It took a lot to pull the wool over his eyes. The next second, he too was gone, his disappearance drawing no attention from anyone.

About the Author

This is the second novel Paul has written in the Festive range, following A Festive Juxtaposition. With three more already written and a sixth book underway the Devil appears to have a good future.

Milton Keynes UK
Ingram Content Group UK Ltd.
UKHW020931181223
434584UK00001BA/41

9 789360 162344